PENGUIN BOOKS
ASCENSION

Eliza Victoria is an award-winning Filipino author. Her books include *Dwellers* (winner of the Philippine National Book Award for Best Novel), *Wounded Little Gods*, the graphic novel *After Lambana* (a collaboration with artist Mervin Malonzo), the science fiction novel-in-stories *Nightfall*, the short story collection *Seventeen Prayers to the Many-Eyed Mother*, and the poetry collection *What Comes After*. She has had stories and poetry published in various venues since 2007, most recently in *The Best Asian Speculative Fiction*, *The Apex Book of World SF*, *Future SF*, *Multispecies Cities*, and *Asian Literature Project*. Visit her at elizavictoria.com.

ASCENSION

Eliza Victoria

PENGUIN BOOKS
An imprint of Penguin Random House

PENGUIN BOOKS

Penguin Books is an imprint of the Penguin Random House group of
companies whose addresses can be found at
global.penguinrandomhouse.com

Published by Penguin Random House SEA Pte Ltd
40 Penjuru Lane, #03-12, Block 2
Singapore 609216

First published in Penguin Books by Penguin Random House SEA 2024

10 9 8 7 6 5 4 3 2 1

This is a work of fiction. Names, characters, places and incidents
are either the product of the author's imagination or are used fictitiously,
and any resemblance to any actual person, living or dead, events or
locales is entirely coincidental.

ISBN 9789815162004

Typeset in Garamond by MAP Systems, Bengaluru, India

www.penguin.sg

For dear friends

Contents

Part I

Imago Mundi

'That woman's staring at you.'

Emilia looked up from her phone at Michelle, who was now looking straight ahead at the hospital clerks clacking away at their computers. The digital sign above the clerks said PATH & LAB RELEASE NOW SERVING 00141 00142 00143. Michelle looked at the piece of paper folded between her fingers—00150—and sighed.

'What did you say?' Emilia said.

Michelle tilted her head to the right. Emilia followed the gesture and saw a woman sitting against the wall near the door, right next to the security guard manning the machine that spat out the numbers for the patients picking up their lab results.

'Do you know her?' Michelle asked.

The woman looked as if she came straight from work, like them, slipping out of the office for a quick fifteen minutes that somehow stretched to forty, the queue moving like molasses. She was wearing a white blouse with long sleeves and a black bow tied at the neck. Pearl earrings. Black pants. Heels. Now that Emilia was looking at her, the woman turned away.

'You know you're staring at her now, too, right?' Michelle said as Emilia rose from her seat. 'Where are you going?'

'I think I do know her, actually.' She left her bag with Michelle and walked over to the woman.

Up close, the woman's face was sweaty, her lips pale and cracked, greasy hair sticking in clumps to her forehead—suddenly looking not as crisp and put-together like her corporate clothes.

'Alma?' Emilia said. She sat on the empty seat next to her.

Alma shifted on her seat to face her. They appraised each other for a few seconds, not smiling, not saying anything.

'I didn't know you worked around here,' Emilia said.

Alma nodded. 'I can't believe we haven't bumped into each other until today. It's been a while, hasn't it, Lia?'

No one had called her Lia in what felt like centuries. 'Yes. What are the odds.'

'Who's that?' Alma's gaze flicked to Michelle, the digital board, and back. PATH & LAB RELEASE NOW SERVING 00146. Michelle was about to nod off in her seat.

'We work together,' Emilia said. 'But in different departments. We just got to talking today. Isn't that weird? We never really talked in the office. You know how you wait in line for a long time and suddenly the person next to you becomes your best friend?'

'Is that right.'

'We just had our annual check-up and they had to re-do her blood test.'

'They found something wrong?'

Emilia shrugged. 'I think they just misplaced her sample. This isn't a very good hospital.'

Alma snorted, and Emilia found herself smiling.

'What kind of work do you do?' Alma asked.

'We work in a bank,' Emilia said. 'I'm in graphic design.'

'Flyers? Brochures? That sort of thing?'

Emilia nodded. 'Nothing too exciting.' She pulled a stray thread from her skirt. 'Anyway, how are you?' She remembered where they were. 'You're not sick, are you?'

Alma smiled, but the smile soon shattered, turned into a grimace, as if Emilia's question physically hurt her. Tears formed in the corner of her eyes.

'What are you doing?' Alma said. 'Why are you being so goddamn pleasant? Do you want to ask me what I had for lunch? What I'm planning to do for the weekend?'

Emilia was too shocked to respond. She looked around her to see if this outburst had any witnesses, but everyone else's eyes were glued to the digital board NOW SERVING 00147.

Emilia held out a hand in an effort to placate her. 'Alma—'

'You walk over here,' Alma continued in a soft voice, 'and you expect me to say I've been fine all these years, I've been doing just fine. Is that it? How dare you?'

'Will you stop?' Emilia said. 'Get a hold of yourself. You're making me regret coming over here to talk to you.'

'I've been so lonely,' Alma said, speaking over her. 'It's been so lonely.' She wiped her tears with her fingers. 'You yanked me away from the doorway—'

'Alma,' Emilia said, her voice steely as she was truly angry now. 'No.'

'—and I've been adrift ever since. Everything just feels so pointless—'

'That was just a story we told each other,' Emilia said. 'I can't believe you. It's been years and years—'

'Do you know what Cotard's Syndrome is?' Alma said.

Emilia stopped talking and shook her head. Is that why Alma was here?

'It's a nihilistic delusion. People with Cotard's Syndrome believe they are already dead. There was this woman who believed all her organs had been destroyed, and that her oesophagus had been glued shut. Do you know what she did next? She starved herself to death.'

Emilia felt like crying. 'Alma. Come on.' A desperate idea. 'Why don't we go get dinner after this?'

'Right,' Alma said, almost sneering. 'After years of silence. Now you want to catch up.'

'You were staring at me. I should have just ignored you.'

'Maybe you should have.'

'It was just a story, Alma.' She didn't know what else to say.

'What is prophecy but the imagination changing reality?' Alma said. 'The physical world confines us, but in certain moments, it becomes malleable. A person would believe anything just to feel they still had some influence on their situation, but sometimes, they do. A delusion can lead to self-starvation, for example. Isn't that amazing?'

Emilia needed to look away from Alma's unnerving smile. The digital board now showed PATH & LAB RELEASE NOW SERVING 00150. Michelle was making her way to the counter, giving Emilia a little wave.

'Go on,' Alma said, smile now gone, as though Michelle's little wave was a slap to her face. 'Go on, go on. Go back to your friend.' She wiped sweat off her forehead and tried to smooth back her hair.

Emilia took out her phone. 'Give me your number.'

'You and I both know you'll never call. You have left it all behind you. You think it's a story and that the story is now over. Go on. Live your happy life like Pauline.'

What makes you think I'm happy? she wanted to say, but Alma had already turned away. She stood up just as Michelle approached, holding out Emilia's bag.

'Let's get out of here,' Michelle said. She watched Alma walk away. 'So you did know that woman.'

Emilia took her bag and tried to hide her trembling hands. 'She's just someone I knew from my hometown.'

They were in the middle of discussing which milk tea place to go to when Emilia heard a surprised scream, the clatter of chairs falling. She felt a vacuum form behind her as people rushed to the centre of the Path & Lab waiting lounge. She pushed her way through the gaggle of onlookers as an emergency alert bounced off of the loudspeakers and found Alma face down on the floor.

All over the town of Santa Clara were fields where nature was allowed to go wild. In one of those fields was a house, choked by thorny vines and surrounded by trees so old that they were starting to rot even with their roots buried deep in the earth. The smell of rot was pleasant, even sweet, on the days when the rain fell, the pungent smell of bark mixing with trampled undergrowth. But on bright, humid days, the odour became unbearably sharp, the trees' rotten trunks looking sinister, dangerous.

Before they woke up whatever it was that dwelled alone in that lonely house, before they all got pulled into its orbit, Emilia had asked Pauline who would choose to live there. The foliage was so thick she couldn't imagine stepping through the doorway without cutting herself. Green branches as thick as the arms of grown men had punched through the wooden boards of its walls, rotting like the trees that surrounded it.

It was dusk when Emilia first came upon this house, a black silhouette etched sharply against the orange glow of the disappearing sun, that fading light like the death knell of an explosion.

'Have you heard about the woman who was blinded upon witnessing the sacred?' Pauline said. 'She saw beauty magnitudes beyond what this world can offer, and it burned the surface of her eyes. Like corneal flash burns. The kind of injury you get from radiation. Experiencing the divine is a two-edged sword. Because of our limitations, it can give us great joy, and great suffering.'

Emilia thought of all this as the emergency trolley squeaked through Path & Lab, as the men and women wearing scrubs turned Alma on her back and slid a CPR board beneath her immaculate white blouse. 'Make room, make room,' the guard said. Emilia was hugging her bag as if it were a life raft. She heard herself whisper and was surprised by the sound of her voice, as if she had turned into someone she hardly recognized. 'Wait, I know her,' she said, as the guard touched her arm and Michelle, standing behind her, gently pulled her back. 'I know her, I know her, she just told me she was fine.'

On certain lonely days, Emilia often wondered what she could have done differently—that first instance when the path forked, she could have gone left and on to an undisturbed life but instead went right. What kind of enormous power pushed a person to enter unexplored territory?

She once read a book about an explorer who launched expeditions in the 1900s for twenty years to find a lost city in South America. What kind of enormous power gave a person the certainty of victory, the unwavering belief that the hardship and toil that came with asking the question will lead to the answer? The explorer disappeared with his son in the jungles of Brazil. At what point during their expedition did these men regret their decision? If given the choice, would they have turned back?

Or were they perhaps beyond regret, and questions about choice were moot? Perhaps the explorer set foot in the Amazon and was changed, the way a blade could be reshaped by fire, and the man who emerged now believed a life away from the forest is not a life at all. Then one could see that his final expedition was not an unfortunate accident or a foolish misadventure, but simply a response to his new nature. The expedition could have been delayed by other factors—his son's health, lack of finances, bad weather—but it could not *not* have happened, because his heart would not let him rest.

Was that it then? Alma's heart would not let her rest? The forest had already closed its doors, but she was desperate to go back into the forest.

They tried to jumpstart Alma's heart, but it had stopped beating. The emergency trolley was not able to revive her. 'One of the doctors in attendance would be preparing the death certificate,' said the nurse who had heard Emilia saying that she knew the deceased. The nurse said the hospital had Alma's patient records and had contacted her next of kin.

'Were you two close?' the nurse asked, looking at her and at Michelle, who shrugged.

'I knew her from years back,' Emilia said. 'We're from the same hometown, but we didn't keep in touch. I just happened to bump into her here.'

'I understand how shocking this is.'

'She was fine just a few minutes ago.'

'Yes,' the nurse said. 'Would you like to speak to pastoral care? You can also wait for Alma's family here if you like.'

'They're coming here?'

'Yes, they're on their way now.'

Emilia paused, and then said, 'No.'

'No?' the nurse said, surprised. Michelle, who was sitting next to Emilia, looked up from her phone.

Emilia stood up, shouldered her bag, fixed her hair and the collar of her blouse that had gone crooked. 'No, thank you.'

There were symbols etched deep into the wood of the doorframe. Emilia didn't notice them at first because of the leaves. A blind woman could have felt its grooves, could have read them through her touch if she knew how to read them. But the symbols did not look familiar at all. She searched her memory and found no reference. But how could that be? Even the house resembled the other houses in town.

'A god lives in this house,' Pauline said.

'God lives in this house?'

'*A* god,' Pauline clarified. 'Imagine you are at the bottom of a mountain during a landslide. You pray, or you run, but you know you will be buried no matter what you did. And yet, a landslide can be beautiful if you see it from a safe distance. It is beauty, and inevitability. It is a great force. That is what I mean.'

Emilia still didn't understand.

'Do you remember the machine at the fair from a few years back?' Pauline asked. 'The doll with the glasses and the top hat?'

'Of course.'

'The one that says, "Pick a colour, any colour." The player picks a colour by placing down his coins or chips, and the doll pushes a button to turn the wheel with the eight colours. Wherever the dial stops, that colour wins, and whoever has chosen that colour gets all the money. The doll does not recognize you or judge you. Ask a question and it will give no answer. It has no past, no future. It is divorced from the march of the seasons, like a saint living in sacred time. It lives in the eternal present, and it eternally asks, "Pick a colour, any colour." If you put your coins on the black square, and the dial stops on the black slice on the wheel, it gives you your prize. The doll and the house's inhabitant—they're the same.'

'How do you know all this?'

'It told me.'

'It?'

'It explained it all to me. It said this is the plainest way it can explain it all to me.'

'It?' Emilia asked again. 'But I don't—'

'It's very old. Very, very old. But what does old mean if you are untouched by time?'

The warm evening was a respite from the harsh air conditioning of the hospital lobby, but Emilia felt sweat form on her nape in a matter of seconds. She glanced at her phone. Seven p.m. The milk tea places nearby would have been closed by now.

'Sorry you got roped into all that,' Emilia said. The shock was now being replaced by visceral embarrassment for crying in front of strangers.

'Oh, please don't apologize,' Michelle said. 'I'm so sorry about your friend.'

'She's not really my friend, when you come down to it.' Distancing herself now from the tragedy and the hurt, as she was wont to do. 'I hardly know her.'

'Life is so short,' Michelle said. 'Sometimes we forget that.'

All the usual comforting pleasantries. *Live every day as if it were going to be your last. I know exactly how you feel. She's in a better place now.*

'What a crazy day,' Michelle said, gathering her hair into a bun. 'Do you think you could eat? I'm getting dinner. Do you want to tag along?' She gestured with her car keys to the queue of people waiting for a taxi or Grab car outside the hospital doors. 'You can't wait on another line. And if you didn't stick around to wait for me you wouldn't be in this mess anyway.'

Emilia hesitated. She didn't think she could eat, but the humid heat was making her thirsty. She plucked at her blouse, the fabric sticking to the sweat on her skin.

'I can give you a lift home,' Michelle said. 'Come on. I can't let you go home alone now. What do you say?'

'Whatever it is, it's alone in there,' Emilia had pointed out to Pauline. 'If you are alone for a very long time, it will drive you insane.'

'It's the passage of time that drives you insane,' Pauline said. 'If I place you in a box and tell you that it will only be for a minute—and it does only feel like a minute—wouldn't you emerge from the box unconcerned? Even though the minute was in fact a hundred years? To feel the passage of time—alone—this is what will break you.' She pointed at the house. 'It is outside of time. It is beyond consciousness.'

'What makes you so sure,' Emilia asked, 'that it's not insane?'

Michelle drove a black sedan, the interior as immaculate as a brand-new car, the dashboard clear, save for a tiny Wonder Woman bobble head taped to the spot beneath the rear-view mirror. There were several restaurants around the hospital, but Michelle chose a place thirty minutes away. Emilia saw the kindness in this. The last thing she needed was to sit next to a group of hospital visitors dissecting what happened in Path & Lab in minute detail.

The restaurant had a corrugated steel door, attractive servers who could not speak (or pretended they could not speak) Tagalog and only spoke English with an American accent, and a menu prohibitively expensive enough to keep several tables empty. Emilia looked over the menu—Japanese–American–Filipino fusion—and let Michelle order. Emilia went with her tried-and-tested conversation starter: 'So how's work going?' She had asked something similar when Michelle had sidled up to her and started chatting while they were waiting at Path & Lab. People liked talking about themselves, and she could go the entire night just nodding and taking a sip of water while the other person talked about their job, their family, their misadventures. It had served her well in the past, after she had left Santa Clara. After she had left Alma, and everyone else.

Michelle said she was training to be a stockbroker—'Can you believe it? Me, a stockbroker!'—and would be taking her SEC Certification Exam soon.

'Does this mean you're leaving the bank?'

'I'm not sure yet,' Michelle said. 'But it's always good to have an exit strategy.'

Emilia thought she should keep deflecting before Michelle could start asking personal questions. 'I don't think I've asked how you ended up at the bank. What was your major?'

This went on for thirty minutes, as Michelle demolished the appetizers—meatballs with an edamame dip—compared each other's main courses, looked over the cocktail menu.

Michelle would be driving, so she just ordered another Sprite. Emilia got herself a whiskey sour.

'Do you enjoy your work?' Michelle asked. 'You're in Corp. Comm., aren't you?'

Emilia glanced at the time. Were Alma's parents already inside the hospital, viewing her body in the morgue?

Her head buzzing with whiskey, Emilia said, without thinking, 'Have you ever had a moment where you felt that nothing you do is of any real importance?'

Michelle looked taken aback. 'Oh. What do you mean?'

What are you doing? 'I work as a graphic artist,' Emilia continued, 'and I enjoy the work. I really do. When I'm working on an illustration, I don't think about its place in the grand scheme of things. It's a shape and I have to shade it. It's a line and I have to stretch it. It's a piece and I have to finish it. It's only when I step back that I—' She took a deep breath. 'I remember sitting in a meeting with one of the VPs, talking to us about deadlines, about using the right brand colour, and I swear I could have stood up and screamed. So what if the Annual Report arrives late? So what if the colour of the cover is a shade too dark? So what? I have a colleague whose wife is dying of lung cancer. Did I tell you about this? He was in that same meeting, because of course he still had to go to work. But I can just imagine what he was thinking. This is important, the asshole VP says, while this man's wife wastes away on a hospital bed. Important?' Emilia laughed, disgusted. 'But I know the dying lives on a different plane.' *Just stop talking.* 'You know the concept of profane time and sacred time?'

'Sure,' Michelle said, looking unsure.

'The man's wife is living in sacred time while her husband and me and that stupid VP continue to live in the time governing ordinary life. We don't live thinking about the grand scheme of things. We live in the everyday. And so the Annual Report *must* arrive on time, the colour of the cover *must* be the correct shade. These are, unfortunately, the things that remain important to us. The dying are sacred, beyond us. It's only the everyday worries of the people they will leave behind that hurt them. Debt, bills, survival.'

Silence. *Now you've done it.* Emilia tried to fight back tears as she finished her drink. *You weird fuck.*

'So,' Michelle asked, 'are you thinking of resigning?'

'What?' Emilia lowered her glass. 'Oh. No. I can't afford to quit. Not just yet, anyway.'

Silence again. Michelle stared at the ceiling, the yellow bulbs twinkling around a painting of a samurai. 'It wasn't your fault,' Michelle said, 'what happened to your friend.'

Emilia grabbed a napkin from the table and dabbed at her eyes. Finally, she said, 'It isn't all bad, where I work,' as though they were just continuing their earlier conversation.

Michelle nodded and gave her a small smile.

'Sometimes I feel tired,' Emilia said. 'Sometimes I feel extremely lucky.'

There was an ethically questionable experiment on avoidance conditioning in the 1960s, where a dog was placed in an apparatus called a shuttlebox. The shuttlebox was divided into two compartments with a hurdle. A light would turn on in the compartment where the dog was standing, and the light would be followed by an electric shock delivered through the floor of the box. The dog could avoid being electrocuted by jumping over the hurdle towards the other compartment. Later, the dog would learn that light equals shock, and would jump right after the light turned on and before the shock could be delivered. The researchers tried this experiment several times, and at some point, turned off the shock generator. But the dog kept jumping.

Researchers had noted that a painful experience equalled a threat to life, and so could change a person more deeply than a pleasurable experience. Emilia found it heartbreaking that a person could be altered not by kindness, but by violence. But she knew it to be true.

She was the person in college who found it physically painful and draining to talk to other people, and so she kept to herself. She was the graphic artist who put on headphones the moment she left her apartment, tuning out everyone and everything else. She was the person who ate lunch at her desk, who said no to birthday parties, to office outings, to drinks. She drank alone, and she drank to be drunk. She feared idle chatter, 'Never Have I Ever', 'opening up', games that forced you to slice open a vein and spill your deepest, darkest secrets. Her greatest fear was to be asked about her childhood, about high school, about her life before she came to the city. She was the dog that kept jumping.

Some survivors of violence forget what it was that had changed them, bestowed with incomplete or false memories. She was not as lucky. Her mind held on stubbornly to that humid evening, as though it were a piece of a puzzle. What was there left to learn? What was there left to learn?

She didn't keep active accounts on any of the social media sites, but Alma did, to her surprise. Another person trying to be someone they were not. Easy-going Alma with the perfect life. Two days after Emilia saw her on the floor of the hospital, her heart suddenly dead and silent, whoever was now managing her Facebook account had posted details about the wake.

'What are you doing?'

Emilia pushed her headphones off one ear. She was sitting at her desk, eating a cheese sandwich she had assembled at home and toasted using the office sandwich press. The Corporate Communications department was empty, save for her, with people partnering up to eat lunch in the cafeteria or outside the building.

Michelle had made her way from Loan Operations and was now peering over Emilia's cubicle, her lavender nails and bright pink wristwatch glinting under the fluorescent lights. 'You're not eating lunch at your desk. It's Friday pay day, for god's sake. Let's try that new Vietnamese place around the corner.'

Emilia took off her headphones and covered her half-eaten sandwich with a napkin. Perhaps it was possible to make a new friend, to create a completely different and beautiful life.

But the Facebook post continued to nag at her, even as they ate their bun cha and drank their iced coffees inside the Vietnamese restaurant, next to a picture window bright with sunlight. Unprompted, Michelle asked if she had heard anything from her friend's family. Her friend who was not really her friend.

'They've taken her home,' Emilia said, showing her the Facebook post. Alma smiling in a summer dress, surrounded by flowers. *Please say a prayer for the eternal repose of—Join us in remembering—*

'Are you thinking of going to the wake?' Michelle scrolled down. 'Oh! Santa Clara. My parents live just a few towns over.'

'Really?'

Michelle handed her phone back to her. 'I'm visiting them tomorrow. I can drop you off, if you want.' Michelle took out her own phone, lavender nails swiping away. 'Wait, are you not on Facebook?'

I'm not sure if I want to go, Emilia thought, but what she ended up saying was, 'It won't be a bother?'

'Dropping you off? No.' Michelle gestured as if writing on air, making calculations. 'From here, we would pass by our town first, then Santa Clara. If you don't mind us stopping at our house first.'

Emilia twirled the remaining vermicelli noodles around her fork. 'What time tomorrow?'

She didn't manage to finish her bun cha, or her cheese sandwich, and brought them both home after work to the three-bedroom apartment she shared with four other women. The kitchen was always messy with ramen packets, the trash can always overflowing with fast-food cups, and there were always pieces of dripping bras and shirts and assorted underwear strung across a makeshift clothesline in the one bathroom that they all shared. But this was better than the arrangements she had seen in other apartments in the same building, where renters were sometimes packed six to a room—three bunk beds squeezed into a room built for one person.

She sat down at the tiny glass table near the door, surveying her life. Two of her housemates were on the sofa, watching a re-run of *The Doctors,* eating grapes from a bowl. Later she would heat up her leftover lunch for dinner. The weekend would pass spent on housework and worrying about Monday, and Monday would come, and it would be another week. Except that the weekend would not just pass this time. Thinking of Alma made her think of Pauline.

You pray, or you run, but you know you will be buried no matter what you did. But Pauline's comparison was flawed, making it seem as if whatever resided in that house was nothing more than a benevolent machine, a tool that shapes itself to its wielder. *If you put your coins on the black square, and the dial stops on the black slice on the wheel, it gives you your prize.*

You put more than coins on the black square.

Maybe it was part of Pauline's trickery, or perhaps she was tricked too? Emilia took out her phone and went straight to Pauline's Instagram page. Her sunlit apartment in Berlin. Photos of her in Dubai, Paris, London, Sydney, New York. She and her parents vacationing in Batanes. Those green rolling hills, that bright blue sky, turquoise waves as far as the eye can see. Emilia had been waiting for the other shoe to drop, because it had to, there had to be a reckoning for all this good fortune. They both left Santa Clara, but Pauline seemed to be happy, thriving, both her parents healthy, while Emilia, friend-less, family-less, worked herself to the bone, living a life among strangers. Perhaps Pauline couldn't sleep at night, but how laughable if that were the extent of her punishment. If that was all. What a small price to pay.

Emilia ate, drank, worked, and slept with her decision, so many years later, and now Alma was dead. What did it matter in the end?

Her two housemates with their bowl of grapes were looking at her. Emilia stood up, wiping her tears with the back of her hand, and locked herself in her room.

Alma visited her at night. Emilia was afraid this might happen.

Here she was now, sitting on the edge of Emilia's bed, wearing the same clothes she was wearing when they last spoke in the hospital. That little bow, the long sleeves that covered her arms up to her wrists. Alma touched Emilia's calf as though to shake her awake, even though she was already wide awake.

'I'm sorry,' Emilia said. What she would give to turn back time. 'I can't help you any more.'

'I was hiding this from everyone,' Alma said. 'Maybe I should show you.'

No, no. Please. You don't have to show me. But Alma was already rolling up her sleeve, and Emilia could see the pink scars left behind by deep wounds. A burn?

'I was trying to get to the muscle,' Alma said, gesturing as if she were holding a knife, carving out patches of skin.

'Why?' Emilia said.

'To look like her.'

'Who?' Emilia asked, even though she knew.

Emilia woke up too early and couldn't go back to sleep, the filaments of her dream covering her like spiderwebs she couldn't swat away. She was ready a full hour before Michelle was supposed to arrive. She sat in the shade on the steps of her apartment building, scrolling through Pauline's feed until she got sick of the meticulously art-directed shots of blooming house plants, champagne flutes, Broadway tickets, sunsets in a foreign city. A car honked, and when Emilia looked up, she saw not Michelle behind the wheel, but a black goat.

It was only for a split-second, but the look on Emilia's face must have been terrifying because it made Michelle jump in her seat. 'God. Are you okay?'

It took Emilia a few tries before she could speak. 'I'm okay,' she finally said. 'I was just thinking of something.' She put on her seatbelt and smiled at Michelle, who was not a black goat but a woman doing her a kindness.

Michelle leaned across the steering wheel and peered up at her building. On the first floor was a busy McDonald's, a Mercury Drug store, a laundry shop. 'You rent here? Damn. This place is expensive.'

'I share the apartment with other girls.' Emilia put on her sunglasses. 'And it just looks nice on the outside. Believe me.'

Michelle talked about the shitty rooms she had rented over the years: the roach-infested one in UP Bliss, the one that didn't have a window in Tomas Morato, the one that got flooded and where her shoes and appliances got ruined in Marikina, and finally, after she decided to move south to Makati so she could be closer to her workplace, a studio apartment on Yague Street. 'It's near Shopwise, so I guess that's a win in this life, you know?'

Michelle turned on her music as they crawled along EDSA. 'What kind of music do you listen to?'

'Oh, I'm fine with anything,' Emilia said, hearing the words and feeling annoyed with herself. *Why can't you have a personality? Why can't you at least pretend?* She tried to recall snatches of conversations among her housemates, her co-workers. 'Taylor Swift?'

Michelle gasped with delight. 'Girl after my own heart.' She switched to a playlist, and Emilia felt pleased to receive this stamp of approval.

Michelle sang along under her breath until they reached the expressway and a phone call cut through the music. It was Michelle's mother, checking if she *really* was coming home for the weekend or if this was another empty promise. 'Ma, I'm literally on NLEX now,' Michelle said. 'A friend's stopping by for lunch. Say hi, Em.' But before Emilia could say a word, they were interrupted by barking. Michelle groaned.

'Michael's home, too? Tell him he better get his smelly dog away from me.'

A tinny voice in the background: 'She's not smelly.'

'Give her another bath!' Michelle said.

She and her mother spoke for another minute before Michelle ended the call, letting Taylor Swift sing again. 'I like dogs, but not that dog,' Michelle said. A brilliant smile. 'Do you have any siblings?'

'No.'

'Ooh, an only child,' Michelle said. 'Are you close to your parents?'

Emilia wondered if she should just say yes and change the topic, but she decided on an answer that would put an end to the conversation. 'Both of my parents are dead.'

A bus zoomed past them, making Emilia flinch.

'Oh.' Michelle glanced at her. 'I'm so sorry.'

'That's okay,' Emilia said, looking out the window. 'Thank you.'

Michelle had stopped singing along with her playlist. She pulled over in front of a 7-Eleven, next to a bus full of children and parents in the final moments of its stopover. The school's name was on the windshield. The bus conductor was calling out the time. Leaving in five minutes. They watched children walk up the bus, hands wrapped around Slurpees. 'Remember school excursions?' Michelle said, smiling at them.

There were families, friends, stepping out in groups from the restaurants. A group of long-haired girls burst through the glass doors of the 7-Eleven, laughing about something. They were all wearing sunglasses. Michelle pulled out her pair from her jeans pocket and put them on. Her sunglasses were reflective; when Emilia looked at Michelle's eyes, she saw only herself. Michelle smiled wider. 'I wish we could get beer, but I think coffee's a better choice.'

Emilia followed her into the store, as though afraid to lose her. Michelle paid at the counter, waving away Emilia's cash. They cracked open their canned coffee drinks outside and drank with their hips resting against the trunk of the car. There was a child jumping up and down inside the bus.

'Those parents are going to regret those Slurpees,' Michelle said, making Emilia laugh.

She felt almost happy, until she remembered where she was going.

Back on the expressway, down an exit, then a right turn before the Bulacan Provincial Hall. Paved road through rice fields. Left turn, then Paombong, the roads growing narrower. Made even narrower by the tricycles parked haphazardly on the sidewalk. Emilia looked closely at them through the windshield.

'Everything looks the same, doesn't it?' Michelle said. 'Nothing ever changes here.'

They went through a gated subdivision, Michelle saluting the security guard at his post, giving a small wave to a man washing his car on the street. She parked in front of a house that was lifestyle-magazine beautiful, all wood and glass and stone veneer. 'Just a warning about my mother,' Michelle said as they stepped out of the car. She popped open the trunk and took out a small gym bag, a basket of fruits. 'She can be a bit much.'

The inside of the house had the same neutral palette as the façade, but it was exploding with energy—Michelle's mother sweeping into the living room with bangles and pearl earrings and a gold crucifix, a Maltese dog yapping in a corner, Michael on the sofa with eyes trained on the TV as he played a loud and violent video game.

'Turn that down,' Michelle said, 'and turn your dog down.'

'Anak,' Michelle's mother said, 'I told you to bring home fresh flowers, not fresh fruits. We already have so much fruit in the house.'

'Thank you for the thoughtful gift, Michelle,' Michelle said, deadpan. 'Glad you got home safe, Michelle. Would you like to have some lunch?'

'Will you stop being rude in front of your friend?' Michelle's mother turned to Emilia and gave her a huge smile. 'Anak, you make yourself feel at home, ha. *Pasensya ka na* with these two. No, no, you don't need to take off your shoes. Come with me. The bathroom's just here if you need to use it. Michael, what did I say about taking Lilith for a walk? She's getting restless.'

Lilith zoomed across the wooden floor and squeezed her way between Emilia's legs, startling her.

'*Diyos ko*, this dog.' Michelle's mother picked the Maltese up and walked to the dining room with the dog in her arms.

'Your home is so beautiful,' Emilia said, as Michelle and Michael fake-punched each other.

Their mother shook her head at them and smiled at Emilia. 'Thank you, anak. Too bad you won't be able to meet my husband. He's in Cebu on a business trip.'

'But he's coming home tomorrow, right?' Michelle asked.

'Yes, he is.'

'I'd like some danggit.'

'And here I am thinking you just miss your Papa.'

The maid set the table with rice, a bowl of fruit—Michelle's mother gestured dramatically towards it and rolled her eyes, as if to say, You see?—*kare-kare*, a bottle of spicy bagoong, and bulalo.

The family talked all throughout lunch, in between urging Michelle to give Emilia more rice or more soup or more water. Emilia was happy to just sit quietly in her corner with her small bowl of hot bulalo, letting the conversations wash over her, mesmerized by the paintings of flowers on the wall, the coal-black accents popping through the white and beige walls, the sunlight streaming through the soft peach curtains, the sight of a family who loved each other. Then Michelle said, 'We work at the same bank, did I tell you, Ma?' and all eyes turned to her.

'Oh, do you?' Michelle's mother said.

'Are you planning to be a stockbroker, too?' Michael asked, pointing at his sister with his fork. 'This idiot's got this bright idea.'

'No,' Emilia said, 'but I think it's a good idea, actually.'

Michelle stuck out her tongue at her brother.

'Are you staying here tonight, anak?' Michelle's mother grabbed a huge dollop of bagoong from the bottle and smeared it on Michael's plate, to his visible dismay. 'We have an extra room.'

'Oh, no, I have to—'

Emilia abruptly stopped speaking, making everyone look up from their plates. Michelle tried to come to her rescue. 'She's going home today, Ma. I'm driving her there after lunch.'

'Why the hurry?' Michelle's mother said. 'She can stay for a few more hours. Michelle, you show her the garden.'

'I can't,' Emilia heard herself speak. 'I have to—' She could feel her carefully constructed self crumbling as the family looked on in wonder, then in shock. 'My friend died.'

Emilia pushed back her chair, making it squeak against the floor, and walked as quickly as she could to the bathroom before she burst into tears. She could hear Michelle back in the dining room saying, '*Ikaw kasi!* With all your questions!' and her mother protesting that she didn't know, anak, you could have sent me a text to warn me beforehand, you know.

Emilia sat on the toilet cover, taking a deep breath to steady herself. A tentative knock. 'Em?' Whispers, Lilith yapping, Michelle's mother telling her to leave her friend alone for a few minutes.

'Em,' Michelle said, a little louder now. 'I'll just be in the living room. Okay? Take your time.'

Emilia splashed her face with water over and over, but her eyes still looked red and swollen. She toyed with the idea of stepping out with her sunglasses. Would they find that strange? But what's stranger than a woman suddenly crying over a bowl of bulalo?

Emilia stashed her sunglasses away and stepped out of the bathroom. The living room was quiet. Michael must have spirited Lilith away. Michelle and her mother were on the sofa, hands folded on their laps, as though they were in the waiting lounge of a clinic, bracing themselves for devastating news.

They both stood up when she appeared. Michelle's mother looked crushed. 'Pasensya ka na, anak. I was asking too many questions. I didn't mean to—'

Michelle cut her off with a glare and shooed her away. Michelle's mother flashed a tense smile at Emilia and disappeared into the kitchen.

'Sorry about Ma,' Michelle said.

'No,' Emilia said. 'She's really nice. Sorry about all that. I didn't mean to—'

Michelle waved her apology away. 'Shall we go?'

Finally, a reason to put on her sunglasses and hide her swollen eyes. 'Let's go.'

Michelle lingered with her mother by the doorway, gesturing to Emilia that she could wait in the car, just give me one second. The sky was clear, and the sun was out, hot rays beating down on the concrete. Emilia sat in the car with the air conditioning blasting straight at her face. Her eyes smart behind the sunglasses. She felt like sleeping. She felt like dying.

She watched Michelle and her mother speak, glance towards the car, speak some more. Then Michelle bid her mother goodbye with a kiss on the cheek, and she was back in the driver's seat, turning the air con vent towards her neck. 'Good God, it's hot as hell.'

'I wasn't able to thank your mother for lunch,' Emilia said. Michelle's mother gave the car a small wave as they pulled out of the driveway.

'Don't worry about it,' Michelle said. 'How are you heading home, by the way? I mean, back to the city. Afterwards?'

'I can take the bus,' Emilia said.

'I'm thinking,' Michelle said, manoeuvring a turn, 'why don't I accompany you at the wake? That way, we can head back here together, and you can meet my father.'

Michelle smiled as though the idea had just occurred to her. 'Have some danggit. Doesn't that sound like fun?'

Emilia was positive this was her mother's idea, a plan hatched earlier at the doorway, but was touched and amused nonetheless by Michelle's effort to appear casual. She was surprised by the tenderness she felt.

'You didn't have to do that.'

'I mean, it's weird,' Michelle said. 'I was there when your friend died. I wouldn't mind paying my respects, you know?'

When was the last time she got invited to another family's home, and a happy one at that? '*Pagpag*,' Emilia said. 'We need to do that. A quick stop before coming back here. You wouldn't want spirits following you home.'

'Oh, there's a shitty Starbucks around the corner,' Michelle said. 'I would happily bring them all the bad juju, don't you worry.'

It had been so long ago, and Emilia was hopeless with directions. Michelle turned on the GPS as Paombong retreated in the rear-view mirror.

'Have you ever been to this part of town before?' Emilia asked.

'Not really,' Michelle said. 'I don't have a lot of friends around here. I feel more at home in the city.'

The car's GPS had gone haywire. *Turn right—turn left—make a U-turn—turn left.* Michelle reached down to switch it off.

'Let's turn left here,' Emilia said. 'This looks vaguely familiar.'

There were no signs, no welcome arch. The asphalt ended and they came upon an unpaved road, lined on either side by wild vegetation. Michelle changed gears, drove slowly, moving like an animal expecting to be attacked. The road was growing ever narrower, the trees closing in.

'Oh,' Michelle said, peering past the wheel. 'I think I see a house.'

The field and the house reminded Emilia of the 3D tilt cards she used to collect as a child. Viewed from one angle, the photo was a forest; viewed from another angle, a T-Rex pops out in the landscape. From one angle, a wild field; from another, a house sitting in the shadow of a clump of trees, choked by vines.

Behind and around the house, there was nothing but vibrant, twisted green.

Emilia glanced once at the house and away, as though the sight of it physically hurt her.

'Wait,' she said.

'There's a tiny house there,' Michelle said, peering, then pointing. A slash of brown through the green.

'We shouldn't have gone down this road,' Emilia said.

'Maybe we can ask for directions.'

'No,' Emilia said. 'We should have taken a different road.'

'Are you okay?'

'I don't think anyone lives there.'

The field was completely silent. No trills, no chitters, no chirps, no whirs. Michelle looked at her face and almost laughed. 'Come on, scaredy-cat,' she said. 'It's worth a shot.' Teasing. 'I'll protect you, I promise.'

Michelle alighted from the car. Emilia had no choice but to follow her. Michelle walked down an incline, stretching her arms on either side for balance, and waded into the knee-high grass.

Michelle started to make her way to the house. Couldn't she see the tree trunks growing in and out of this abomination? How could anyone believe anyone lived there?

'Wait,' Emilia said. Her legs felt heavy.

But Michelle was already at the door, which was wide-open. Inside, they could see the shadow of a woman, lit by slashes of sunlight streaming through the gaps between the wooden planks that made up the house's walls. Her silhouette suggested unruly hair, a house frock a size too big for her body. A black veil.

'Hello?' Michelle said.

Emilia breathed hard, trying to hold on, trying not to pass out. Trying hard not to scream. She reached out to grab Michelle's wrist.

No answer. No movement. They could not see the inhabitant's face. There was a putrid smell coming from her—the smell of vomit and decay.

'I think we should go,' Emilia tugged at Michelle's arm. 'Can we go? Please?'

Michelle let Emilia pull her away. 'Okay,' Michelle said, as though placating a scared child. 'Okay, okay, we'll go now.'

'That was so weird,' Michelle said. 'Was that woman wearing a veil?'

Black clouds were forming. They took off their sunglasses. It began to rain in a matter of minutes, the sudden downpour overwhelming the windshield wipers. Michelle took her foot off the gas and drove at a crawl.

'Does she live there?' Michelle kept saying, as though faced with a puzzle she wanted to solve right away. Michelle glanced at Emilia. 'Are you okay?'

Emilia's heart was hammering inside her chest. 'Should we just turn back?' she whispered.

Michelle, not dissuaded, peered through the sheet of water out the passenger-side window. 'Do you see anything?' she asked. 'If you see another house, will you let me know? We'll get to the wake, don't you worry.'

All Emilia could see were trees, but after a while the narrow road opened up, and they came upon a fork. When Michelle asked which way they should turn, Emilia said, without hesitation, 'Turn right.'

'You remember now?' Michelle said, delighted.

'I guess so.'

Immediately, they came upon houses, one after the other, standing right on the edge of the road, women in a flurry as they grabbed clothes from clotheslines. Children's faces appeared behind small windows, watching the rain.

'Here we go,' Michelle said. 'Civilization.'

They saw houses that were built farther back from the road. These were bigger houses on bigger lots, with enough space for a garden, or a front yard, or a driveway.

They passed by a two-storey house and saw a man sitting on a flimsy plastic chair on the front porch, smoking a cigarette.

'This is Alma's family home,' Emilia said.

Emilia thought of rolling down the window and calling out a greeting, but realized the sound of the rain would just drown out her voice. They needed to get closer.

The man, who was wearing jeans and a fitted black shirt, looked nonplussed. He didn't get up from his stoop, and just watched them, smoking, as Michelle manoeuvred the car onto the property.

Now at shouting distance, Emilia rolled down her window and said, 'Good afternoon!'

The man pulled a long drag on his cigarette, just staring at them, as though memorizing their faces. After a moment, he stood up, dropped his cigarette on the wet ground, and walked into the house.

'What?' Michelle said in surprise. 'How rude.' But seconds later the man stepped out of the door, now under a large, black umbrella.

He walked up to the car and bent down to peer into the driver's seat. He was about to say something to Michelle but glanced past her and locked eyes with Emilia.

The rain had obscured his face, but now she could see him clearly. 'Lucas,' she said with a smile. Alma was a surprise, a mirage out of context, but here Lucas was where she last left him, just smoking a cigarette, and not spouting nonsense about a forgotten time.

Now Lucas could see her clearly too. He didn't seem as pleased. He looked almost heartbroken. 'Lia,' he said. 'You came back?'

Emilia shrugged. 'Just for the wake.'

'Wow,' he said. 'I thought we'd never see you back here again.'

We.

Michelle had turned her face away from Lucas and was mouthing, 'He's cute.'

Emilia suppressed a laugh. 'Lucas, this is Michelle.'

'Nice to meet you!' Michelle said brightly, shaking his hand through the car window. Lucas mirrored her wide smile, but he gave Emilia a look she couldn't quite read.

'Come on, everyone's inside,' he said. 'You can have this umbrella.'

Lucas ran to the porch while Michelle and Emilia shared the umbrella. Emilia walked slowly, like a person half-asleep.

Coming in from the grey light and the cold wind, the house felt like a dark sauna, filled with people standing against the wall carrying plates of food or sitting on the same flimsy plastic chairs that Lucas had been using. Heads began to turn as Emilia pushed the door open and Michelle wrestled with the dripping umbrella. The coffin was silver with a hint of blue, brightly lit, surrounded by stands of flowers bearing the names of the families who had sent them. The photo that they used for Alma's Facebook memorial page had been blown up, now seated on an easel next to the flowers.

The living room was not built to house the dead and her mourners. It felt cramped, it felt wrong, and Emilia was starting to feel faint from the heat. As though reading her mind, Lucas said, 'Let's move to the back, there's more room there,' and so they moved to the back, towards the kitchen. Cool air blew in from the back door, and Emilia could see that they had set up tents and tables in the backyard, where several people were seated, playing cards in earnest.

'Would you like a coffee?' Lucas was already ripping open a coffee packet.

'Sure, thanks,' Michelle said, cheerful and eager. Emilia was amused by Michelle's sudden enthusiasm for instant coffee. Lucas poured hot water from a battered and scratched lime-green thermos. The mugs, with small chips on the handles, had also seen better days. Emilia's own mother would have bent over backwards to bring out the good china for visitors, but perhaps there was no good china. Perhaps Alma's parents couldn't be bothered because their only child was dead.

'I didn't see Alma's parents,' Emilia said.

'They're upstairs,' Lucas said. 'I don't think *Tita* Cristina has stopped crying ever since,' he shrugged, 'you know.'

There was someone, dry-eyed, who kept running from the kitchen to the living room, continuously refilling the baskets of candy and bread and instant coffee packets despite Alma's aunts and uncles telling him to slow down, let them help. He bore their embraces and commiserations as he would a monotonous school lecture. Emilia could almost see him drumming his fingers. Was it one of Alma's cousins?

Lucas cornered him in the kitchen. 'Look who I found.'

'Joaquin,' Emilia said, when she finally saw his face. She lifted a hand and gave him a small wave.

Joaquin was about to carry more mugs of coffee for the men playing cards outside when Lucas stopped him. He paused for a moment, staring at Emilia. 'You're here,' he said, with quiet wonder. But then he seemed to remember the tray he was carrying. 'I'll be right back.'

When he returned to the kitchen, Emilia introduced him to Michelle. While Lucas was fair-skinned with the Chinoy features that Michelle seemed to favour, Joaquin had big, black eyes that made him look mischievous, like a child planning a prank. Several of his fingers were wrapped in adhesive bandages.

Lucas put down his mug. 'I should take over, shouldn't I?'

Joaquin scoffed. 'It's fine, they can get their own coffee. Let's stay with the girls for a bit.' He turned to Michelle, 'We're all old friends.'

'So I gathered,' Michelle said. She nudged Emilia with her shoulder. 'That's nice, having a little group of friends growing up.'

The word 'nice' hung heavy in the air and fell in the room like dead weight.

Emilia broke the awkward silence. 'Are you still working at the butcher shop?' she asked, gesturing towards Joaquin's hands.

He nodded.

'With your father?' Emilia asked. 'Still?'

It was very subtle, the twitch in the corner of his eye, but Emilia saw it. 'Not any more,' he said. 'My father died five years ago.'

Emilia nodded. 'I'm sorry,' she said, not feeling sorry at all. 'If you don't mind me asking, how did he die?'

'Stupid accident.' He shrugged. 'Keeled over while blind drunk. He hit his head.'

Emilia filed this new information away to look it over later. 'So you run the shop now.'

'Big businessman,' Joaquin said with a wry smile. 'That's me.' He pointed a thumb at Lucas. 'And this one's teaching at the college.'

'Here?' Emilia said. 'I thought you were going to teach at UP.'

'Turns out it's not for me, city girl,' Lucas said.

'He'd like to contain his corruption of young minds within the town limits,' Joaquin said.

Lucas chuckled. 'Accurate.'

'Have you visited Sophie?' Joaquin asked. He turned to Michelle to explain. 'That's another friend of ours, but she mostly stays at home.'

'She's sickly,' Lucas added.

'No, I haven't seen her,' Emilia replied.

Joaquin sipped his coffee. 'If you're staying in town a bit longer, we can walk there. I'm sure she'd love to see you.'

'So, from the group,' Michelle said, 'it's just you and Alma who left town.'

Emilia noticed the curious look Joaquin gave Michelle but didn't comment on it.

'And Pauline,' Emilia added.

Another heavy silence. They could hear the murmurs of mourners floating in from the living room.

'How did you know Alma again?' Joaquin asked Michelle.

Before Michelle could answer, Emilia found herself blurting out, 'Alma collapsed in front of us when we were in the hospital.'

Lucas and Joaquin looked at each other, a quick glance.

'That was you?' Lucas said.

'We heard what happened from Tita Cristina,' Joaquin said, 'but we never realized you were there.'

'Did Alma,' Lucas ventured, stopped. Then: 'Did Alma say anything to you?'

Emilia felt the tears falling. She hated this, hated herself. She was doing so well, smiling and laughing at the right moments, moving the conversation away from dangerous territory, but now all she could hear was Alma saying, *I've been so lonely, it's been so lonely.*

'Oh, shit,' Lucas said.

'Now look what you've done,' Joaquin said, placing an arm around Emilia. The gentleness of the gesture just made Emilia cry harder. Did she even realize how lonely she had been?

'I think the rain has stopped,' Michelle said. 'Maybe we can sit outside? Get some air?'

'Great idea,' Lucas said, and held the back door open for them so they could shuffle out of the kitchen.

They were in the same grade but belonged to different class sections at the elementary school. They would see each other at the market or at church, but never spoke to each other until the mass panic at school that sent students racing to the Science Garden one Tuesday during recess.

Six students from different grades started screaming inside the garden toolshed, claiming that they had seen a woman wearing a black veil. The students who were out on the grounds during recess surrounded them as they ran out, eager to hear what had happened. It took two hours for the teachers to break up the group. There were fainting spells, panicked crying. No one wanted to go near the Science Garden, and so the teachers had no choice but to suspend the agriculture and botany classes for the day.

At four in the afternoon, the principal called for an emergency assembly and presented one of the original six students, Nico, urging him to tell them what he had told his teachers. 'I made it up,' Nico said. 'I told Ruby that I saw a woman wearing a black veil, but I just said it to scare her. Then she told everyone else in the toolshed with us. I didn't mean to scare everyone.'

The principal praised the student for admitting his wrongdoing and talked a bit about the power of suggestion. 'Sometimes our worst enemy is our own mind,' she said. 'Let today be a lesson for all of you.'

Agriculture and botany resumed the next day, and grade 6 students returned to the Science Garden to tend to their Chinese cabbage and make notes about the bitter gourd plant crawling on the trellises. Emilia, Pauline, Alma, Sofia, and Joaquin had stayed behind after class was dismissed, and walked up to Lucas washing his hands using the faucet outside the dreaded toolshed.

Lucas saw them looking at him through the bars of the fence and asked, 'Do you want to look inside?'

They entered the garden. They stood side by side in front of the toolshed's doorway.

'Do you believe what Miss Santos said?' Emilia asked. 'About the power of suggestion?'

'In 1518, in Strasbourg, people danced for a month without rest,' Lucas said, drying his hands with a white handkerchief, folded into a neat square. 'It started with one woman, Frau Troffea, twirling alone on the street. By August, there were four hundred people dancing.'

'You made that up,' Alma said.

'I did not,' Lucas said. 'I read it in a history book. My father has a lot of books at home.'

Emilia fell silent, reacquainting herself with a world where four hundred people nearly danced themselves to death.

'People in Europe believed in a Catholic saint, St. Vitus, who cursed people with the dancing plague. Maybe Troffea thought she was cursed, and persuaded other people that they were cursed as well. If you believed anything hard enough, you could change reality, I guess.'

'I'm not sure about Nico, though,' Joaquin said. 'He's not smart enough to influence people.'

Lucas laughed. 'So you think he really saw someone?'

They shrugged.

'How about a dare?' Lucas said. 'I dare you all to stay in the toolshed for a full minute.'

'You're coming with us?' Pauline said.

'Sure.'

They stepped through the doorway and entered the toolshed. Gardening tools hung on hooks from the ceiling. Broken armchairs were stacked on top of each other in the dark corners. Emilia knew if she stared at a corner long enough, through the cobwebs and the odd shapes of the broken chairs, she'd be able to make herself see a bird, a man, a woman wearing a dark veil. Anything at all.

'Let's go,' Emilia said. She expected the group to make fun of her for giving up so quickly, but they didn't. They walked with her out of the toolshed without a word.

They were still silent as they left the school together. After a few minutes, Pauline asked, 'Did you smell anything in there? Other than fertilizer, I mean.'

The others shrugged, shook their heads.

Emilia said, 'I smelled perfume.'

Pauline did not comment, and now Emilia was worried, thinking of Nico and the dancing people of Strasbourg. She did smell perfume—a sweet, cloying smell that covered up the smell of manure and was gone in a matter of seconds— but she didn't want to be accused of putting a foolish idea in Pauline's head.

After that encounter at the Science Garden, they would visit each other during the weekends, sometimes even helping Emilia with repacking items for the store. Like Joaquin's father, Emilia's parents ran a store at the Santa Clara Public Market. Her parents sold the same staples as most of the other stores in the market: rice, sugar, flour, garlic, onion, pepper, repacked from wholesale sacks into retail packs.

Other stores made enough money to hire people to do the repacking, but Emilia's family only had her. Now they also had her newfound friends, who would scoop white sugar from the wholesale sack and pour it into plastic bags on top of the weighing scale to make kilo, half-kilo, and one-fourth-kilo packs for retail.

Emilia was fascinated with Lucas, and with the things he found fascinating. Surrounded by sacks of produce in the storeroom, a glass of instant orange juice and liver-spread sandwiches at his elbow, Lucas would talk about the Black Death, the disease spread more rapidly by rat fleas living in the clothes of people and on the ships fleeing a plague-stricken town. It took people weeks before they realized an epidemic was upon them. Before long they were burying dead bodies every day.

'People lost their respect for the Church,' he said. 'They either blamed the Church for not protecting them against the Black Death, or they thought there was something wrong with the Church itself that led to Europe being punished by God. Bodies were buried in mass graves, which was against the teachings of the Church, but even the clergy had no choice because there were so many dead bodies. They just didn't know what to do any more.'

Lucas would take them to his father's home office, where his father kept his books and old teaching props—human anatomical models, plastic skeletons, biology lab kits—and show them photos of the flagellants who broke away from the Church and sought shelter from divine wrath by publicly whipping themselves with a scourge.

'A person would believe anything,' he said, 'just to feel he still had some influence on his situation.'

Emilia imagined her parents with lymph nodes swollen to the size of chicken eggs, imagined herself digging up the wet soil of their backyard for their graves. What she would sacrifice to avoid such a fate.

Lucas enrolled at the private high school where his father taught, taking advantage of the tuition scholarship offered to children of faculty. The others enrolled in the public high school across the road. Lucas' high school, ran by Catholic priests, had a programme where their students would visit the public high school to teach a subject they simply called 'Religion'.

'And by Religion, you mean Catholicism,' Emilia said during one of these programmes, all of them sitting with Lucas at the back. Lucas was in charge of the visual aids. His classmate at the front of the classroom was talking about Abraham and Isaac, holding up a copy of Caravaggio's *Sacrificio d'Isacco*, which Lucas had printed in colour. Abraham's thumb on Isaac's cheek as he pressed his head against the stone altar, the angel gripping Abraham's wrist, stopping the knife. 'And by Catholicism, you mean Bible stories.'

'And by Bible stories,' Lucas said, gesturing at their homeroom teacher nodding off at her desk, 'I mean teacher's recess.'

Beyond these visits, they would meet every now and then: at the public market, where their parents worked or where they bought groceries, or on the way home after their classes.

One big news story they heard growing up was of a high school student in the city who went to several churches—*Visita Iglesia*—praying to pass the college entrance exam to his dream university. On his way to the last church, he was stabbed to death in a robbery.

Emilia brought it up with Lucas.

'He did actually get into his dream school, you know,' he said. 'UP. He even got into a quota course. Business Administration and Accountancy.'

'So his prayer worked?' Emilia said.

'Shit happens.'

'Shit happens. That's it?' A sad chuckle. 'The murderer with the ice pick happened,' Emilia said.

'It's actually even simpler,' Lucas said. 'The human body happened. Question: Why did he die? Answer: A man stabbed him and left him bleeding to death. True, but also: Because he got stabbed in the lung, and in the liver, and the blade nicked an artery in his heart, and the wounds caused damage so catastrophic that his body couldn't recover. Everything we are, are in this complex mass of grey matter in a hard shell, but the hard shell's so easy to break. You hit your head a certain way and you lose your ability to speak. One moment you're singing, the next moment you're a piece of meat. Human life is precious and fragile, but people only focus on its being precious.'

'God should have made us indestructible then,' Emilia said.

'Which would lead to a radically different experience of life,' Lucas said. 'Which would lead to a radically different you. To a not-you. Life is a fragile gift, but it's what we're given. Why be angry when you can be grateful?'

'So shit happens,' Emilia said, 'but just be happy you're alive?'

Lucas shrugged. 'What else is there to do?'

She would think about this exchange during her darkest days in the years to come.

Emilia's parents were always knee-deep in produce, wholesale sacks forming a border around the store, leaving space only big enough for three or four people, and a desk with drawers of bundled cash, on top of which rested a small television and a dusty electric fan barely stirring the humid air. The customers would often just stand behind this border and hand over their grocery lists so Emilia and her parents could squeeze past each other and pack the orders into plastic bags or boxes.

Pauline and her mother were waiting for their orders. Emilia willed her parents to work faster. She liked Pauline just fine, but Pauline's mother was loud and seemed to feel it was her duty to fill every lull in every conversation. Right now, she was going on a rant about the rallies in the city. It was the summer of 2006, and the top news item was the abduction of three university students conducting research in Santa Clara, allegedly by the military, allegedly because they were—

'Communists,' Pauline's mother said, spitting out the word as if it were poison, shaking her head. Emilia glanced at their small TV. She watched the students in the city marching with placards, screaming at the line of policemen wearing riot gear, demanding that the military release the abducted students. 'These children have been brainwashed by the Communists,' Pauline's mother continued, while Emilia's parents solemnly nodded. 'Their parents are breaking their backs to pay their tuition. They should have mercy on their parents!' She turned to Emilia and Pauline. 'Now you—' and here both she and Pauline shared a look and tuned out, because they already knew the gist of this particular speech: study well, get good grades, get a scholarship, go to university, find a good job—hopefully abroad, where the pay was better—and help their poor, suffering parents.

'What if Ate Mia joined a rally?' Pauline said, cutting her tirade short. Emilia hid her smile. Pauline's older sister, Mia, was attending university in the city, studying to become a doctor.

Her mother looked affronted. 'Your sister would never!'

Emilia had found it strange to hear the name of their hometown emerge from the newscaster's mouth, to read it with the headlines crawling at the bottom of the screen. Whenever she passed by the church or walked to the market, she would see men in military uniform setting up checkpoints. They never had checkpoints or any form of military presence in town before. The soldiers made her feel anxious, even though she had not done anything wrong.

No one Emilia knew, including her parents, teachers, and friends, lost any sleep over the abducted students in Santa Clara. If they were Communists, they thought, then that meant they endorsed armed insurrection against the government. They were no innocents, they knew what they were getting into, they got what they deserved. The military men were just doing their jobs. Even the priests at church never mentioned them in their sermons, never asked the parishioners to pray for their safety, as the offertory basket made its way around the pews.

The students turned up two weeks later, arms and legs bound with rope, heads wrapped in packaging tape, their bodies bobbing up and down in the Santa Clara River. More protests exploded in the city, some of them turning violent.

Mia did end up joining one of the rallies, and she got hit by a truncheon. Emilia knew this because Pauline's mother wouldn't stop talking about it. 'She came home with seven stitches in her head,' she said while Emilia prepared her orders—kilo of rice, kilo of sugar, half-kilo of onions, three heads of garlic—arranging them in her basket. 'Seven stitches, can you imagine? Why would she even involve herself in this? I told her, "Look at you, with that wound in your head. Do you think you made a difference, shouting at police and stopping traffic?"'

Whenever Emilia passed by the river now, she would choose a wild flower from the banks and throw it into the water, as if the Santa Clara River were a vast offertory basket, and the flower was all the riches she could impart. She didn't know exactly what it was she was praying for. Safety? Mercy?

One time, she forgot to do it, hurrying after her parents after Sunday Mass. When she remembered the river, it hit her like a physical blow, and her hands started shaking. She ran out of the house all the way to the public market, and threw a cluster of red santan flowers into the river when she was sure nobody was looking.

Emilia had not thought about the toolshed for years, until Pauline brought it up one afternoon as they walked home from school.

'Is your sister still home?' Emilia asked. She didn't know Mia that well. She was the college girl, an abstraction summoned only during family dinners, a blurry figure flitting in and out of the house during the weekends.

Mia liked teasing Emilia and Lucas whenever she saw them sitting close together with a book in a corner of the living room. Pauline would tell her to shut up and stop bothering her friends, Emilia would bow her head to hide her face, Mia would giggle, and that was the extent of Emilia's interaction with her. But she got worried when she heard that Mia was injured. 'How is she doing now?'

They were walking by the river. There were little boys sitting on the banks, shirtless, skin burning under the afternoon sun, daring each other to jump. Emilia wanted to ask them if they knew about the dead bodies that were fished out of the river just a few weeks ago.

'Do you remember the Science Garden at our elementary school?' Pauline asked, staring at the water. 'Do you remember the toolshed?'

Emilia took a while to home in on the memory. The toolshed, the students screaming about a ghost. 'Yes,' she said. 'But I was asking about Mia.'

'You said you smelled perfume while we were in there.'

'I did,' Emilia said, mystified.

'I did too,' Pauline said. 'I don't think I ever told you.'

Emilia frowned. Why was she bringing this up now?

'I dreamt that something visited me last night,' Pauline said, 'and told me a story.'

'Something?' Emilia smiled a little. Was Pauline pulling her leg? 'What are you talking about?'

Pauline began telling her the story. There was a girl running away from home to find a quiet place to cry, and found an empty house in a field. It was as if the house came out of nowhere. But soon, the girl realized that the house wasn't empty. In the house was a—

Pauline fell silent.

Emilia glanced at her. 'What?'

'Whoever lived in the house,' Pauline continued, 'is beyond comprehension, and that which you cannot comprehend can destroy you. It told her things she was not supposed to know. The girl should have run from the house and never looked back. But she couldn't run fast enough. It was already too late.'

Emilia looked at Pauline with alarm, as though she had just confessed to killing somebody. 'What the hell was that?'

'A story,' she said. 'It also gave me a message that it said would make sense to you.'

'You said it visited you last night?' Emilia said, angry now. Scared. 'What do you mean? What visited you last night?'

'It said you should stop giving flowers to the river,' Pauline said.

Emilia stopped walking. 'What did you say?'

'It said it won't change a thing.' Pauline frowned. 'No. Wait. That's not right. It said, "It's not enough."'

Emilia took a step and felt her knees buckle. Pauline grabbed her just in time. 'So it made sense?' Pauline said. 'The message made sense?'

'You saw me, didn't you?' Emilia's face aglow with realization. *Of course, of course. Everything has a logical explanation.* 'You saw me throw a flower into the river once, and now you're just trying to scare me to death.'

But Pauline's face held a look of grim wonder. 'Let's keep walking,' she said. She cleared her throat, and tried on a buoyant tone that didn't match the look in her eyes. 'It looks like rain, doesn't it?'

Emilia's parents, after hearing that Mia was still at home convalescing, sent Emilia off with a basket of fruits.

Pauline greeted her at the door. It had been a week since she told her the strange story about a strange visitor, but Emilia still felt as if she were standing on uneven ground with her.

'I have to make lunch,' Pauline said. She gestured at the basket of fruits. 'Is that for us? That's nice. You can bring that up to Ate Mia.'

Mia's room was as hot as a furnace. The windows were closed, the curtains drawn, Mia a shapeless bulge beneath the bedsheets. An electric fan stood desolate in a corner. Emilia placed the basket on the floor and opened a window, switched on the fan.

Mia stirred on the bed. Emilia lifted the basket and put it on Mia's study table. She didn't want to talk to her. Mia made her feel awkward. But before she could leave, Mia said, 'Are those flowers for the river?'

Emilia stopped dead in her tracks. Mia sat up, emerging from the sheets. For a person recovering from a head injury, she looked incredibly beautiful, her eyes bright, her lips dark pink, her hair luscious and black on her shoulders. The bandage covering the stitches on her head looked out of place.

'Oh, they're fruits, not flowers,' Mia said, staring right at her, not glancing once at the basket hidden in the shadows. 'Silly me.'

Emilia stood next to the fan. She could feel its base vibrating on the floor. She could feel the cold wall as she pressed against it. 'Ate Mia?'

'I heard you and Pauline talking about the house,' Mia said.

'Oh,' Emilia said, relieved that she was able to finally follow what Mia was saying. 'That's nothing. She was just telling a weird story.' But then: how did Mia hear them talking? They were out there by the river. Did Pauline tell her?

'What is prophecy but the imagination changing reality?' Mia said.

'Lia?'

Pauline opened the door with a plate of food. She glanced at Emilia, then at the bed. 'Oh, she's asleep,' Pauline said.

And Mia was asleep. Greasy hair stuck in clumps to her face, her lips pale and cracked.

'Lia, are you all right?' Pauline asked, but she was distracted, she was already turning away. She failed to notice Emilia's trembling hands, her wide-eyed stare. 'There's food downstairs if you're hungry.'

Mia was dead a day later.

She fell asleep and just didn't wake up.

At the wake, they could hear people mumbling that Mia shouldn't have gone to that rally, such a bright young woman, such a waste, while others kept saying that the police shouldn't have used force at a peaceful protest. Neither argument was winning, at least as far as Mia's mother was concerned, she who liked filling the silence and joining the fray in a fierce debate. None of it mattered now, because her daughter was dead.

'My sister died because of a blow to the head,' Pauline said, when Emilia sat next to her at the wake. The others were keeping their distance, unsure of what to do or say. 'A single blow to the head.'

'Oh, Pau.'

Emilia had heard that Pauline's father, who had had a heart attack last year, took Mia's death hard and was not sleeping at all. He looked visibly weary, face swollen from silent crying, mouth slightly open, sitting stiff as though he were just a mannequin propped up on a chair. Emilia saw someone try to speak to him, and he didn't even look up, didn't even move his head.

They were all worried about his worsening health.

'I've been to a funeral where they put chicks on the coffin,' Pauline continued, 'because the dead person was murdered, and they believed the chicks pecking at the coffin's glass were also pecking at the murderer's conscience. I guess it made them feel better.' Pauline shrugged. 'Do you think my parents can put chicks on my sister's coffin?'

Emilia didn't know what to say.

'I'll meet them soon,' Pauline said.

'Who?'

'Whoever was in the house.'

'What?'

Emilia wished Pauline would cry, like her mother right now, sobbing hysterically next to Mia's coffin. Crying she could understand. Crying she knew how to respond to, but what could she say in response to this? This calmness, this frightening conviction?

Pauline picked at something on her skirt. 'I should be ready.'

Ready for what? 'It's just a story,' Emilia said. 'The house and the girl. Right? You made it up.'

'What is prophecy but the imagination changing reality?'

'What?' Emilia said. She gripped her arm. 'What did you say?'

Pauline looked at her with pity. 'It's okay,' she said. 'You'll see.'

Emilia sat listening to Lucas and Joaquin regaling Michelle with silly stories from their childhood, but not these stories, not these tragedies. Not the ones that mattered. They, too, knew to steer clear of them. Sitting with her friends with a mug of coffee, her shoes splattered with mud, the rain-drenched breeze blowing on her face, Emilia felt almost safe, but still wary. As if she were teetering on the edge of a cliff.

Michelle caught her eye. 'Are you okay?'

Emilia took a beat too long to answer. 'Yes,' she said. 'I'm okay.'

'Do you want something to eat?' Joaquin asked.

She shook her head.

'So tell me about Pauline,' Michelle said. 'I guess she worked in the city, too?'

'She's in the US,' Lucas said. 'Got a full scholarship to go to UP, then she went off to Stanford on a Fulbright.'

'Smart girl,' Michelle said.

'Lucky girl,' Lucas said. He took out his cigarette packet and offered it to the table. No one else smoked. 'Do you mind?' he asked, and proceeded to light the cigarette before they could answer. He moved his chair to Joaquin's right so he would be upwind and smoke wouldn't get in his friend's face.

'She left shortly after her older sister died,' Joaquin said.

'Oh, how sad.'

Emilia took out her phone and showed the screen to Michelle.

'Do you have old pictures in there?' Joaquin asked.

'No, I'm showing her Pauline's Instagram page.'

'Well, la di da,' Michelle whispered as she scrolled. 'Your friend's living her best life.' She whipped her head up, as though caught committing a faux pas. 'But I'm really sorry to hear about her sister.'

'I think Pauline's working as a software engineer,' Emilia said.

'I can't believe you follow her on Instagram,' Joaquin said.

'I don't,' Emilia responded. 'I just check it every now and then.'

'Keeping tabs?' Lucas quipped, smirking.

Emilia looked at him, daring him to say more. Lucas held her gaze, smoking his cigarette. Joaquin took a deep breath, witnessing all this, and exhaled slowly.

Michelle returned the phone. Emilia thought the moment had passed, but Lucas looked visibly irked now.

'Did you know that in our last year of high school, Alma was blind for more than a month?' Lucas told Michelle.

Emilia sat up straight, as though she had been electrocuted.

'No way,' Michelle said.

'Conversion disorder. They used to call it hysterical blindness, but that's an old, sexist term.'

'I didn't know that that can happen,' Michelle said, chin on her hand, engrossed now. 'Like total blindness, but temporary?'

'Do you know why they call it conversion disorder?' Lucas said. 'It's a psychological state converted to a physical symptom. It can present as blindness, or hearing loss, or paralysis. Based on the usual tests, Alma was not blind. I mean, she was, but not *really*. Not medically. There was nothing wrong with her eyes. But asking if she were *really*

blind was irrelevant at that point, because she couldn't see.'
He blew cigarette smoke up towards the tent roof. 'The brain
is a strange thing. Of course, I can only marvel at it after that
whole nightmare, but isn't it amazing how the brain can fool
you? How it can fool itself? It's mind-blowing how there's a
part of you that's somehow also separate from you and the
physical world and all its laws.'

A short silence followed.

'You sound just like Pauline,' Emilia said.

'Oh, sure,' Lucas said. 'Like you've spoken to her recently.
Do you chat with each other on Instagram?'

'No,' Emilia said, feeling heat climb up her face. 'Do you?'

Silence as Emilia and Lucas simmered.

'So what caused Alma's blindness?' Michelle said,
seemingly unperturbed by the blow-up. 'Was it stress?'

'Something like that,' Emilia said.

Lucas laughed in disgust. 'Did you even speak to Alma at
all before you saw her again at the hospital? Before she died
in front of you?'

'Easy, Lucas,' Joaquin said.

Lucas ignored him. 'She went blind, and you just left,' he
said, his voice breaking on the last word, as though he were
about to burst into tears.

'You are unbelievable,' Emilia said, unmoved by this
performance. 'Like you care? You? Innocent guy who has
never hurt anyone?'

'Come on,' Joaquin said, raising his voice a little, hands on
his temples. 'We have a guest here. Sorry about this, Michelle.'

Lucas left the table, kicking a table leg as he stood up.

'Sorry,' Michelle said after a moment.

'No,' Emilia and Joaquin said at the same time.

'I should have just stopped asking my stupid questions.' She pursed her mouth. 'But he's kind of a jerk.'

'*I'm* sorry,' Emilia said. She began to stand up. 'Let me just find Alma's parents and we can get out of here.'

'Wait, come on,' Joaquin said. He followed them as they walked back into the house. 'Let's go visit Sophie, at least. Don't you want to see Sophie?'

'I don't want to put Michelle out more than I already have.'

'No, it's okay,' Michelle said. 'Why don't you say hi to your friend? I can hang back here for a few minutes and—'

Alma's mother was in the kitchen.

Emilia stopped in her tracks so suddenly that Michelle and Joaquin collided into her. Mrs Bartolome was making a cup of coffee, surrounded by relatives urging her to sit down, sit down, why don't you just *sit down*, Tina, rest your feet, we can do that for you.

Mrs. Bartolome's hair had been swept into a perfect bun, no strand out of place, but her eyes were swollen and tender, and there were brown coffee grounds dusting the front of her black dress. 'Anak,' she said, walking up to Emilia and taking her hand. 'They told me you were able to speak to my daughter before—before she—'

'Yes, Tita,' Emilia said.

Mrs Bartolome led her into the living room, to where Alma lay in a coral dress, the colour matching the rouge on her cheeks, the shiny tint on her lips. 'I'm glad you were able to speak to her before—' She couldn't seem to bear to say it. 'You haven't seen each other in so many years.'

'We just talked about work, what she's been up to,' she said. 'I know I haven't been by to visit.'

'Oh, you were all busy. Living your life.'

What else could she say that wouldn't cause another wound? 'She said she was very happy,' Emilia said.

The rain and wind had died down, but it was still chilly, the sky grey and dull. Emilia and Michelle stood side by side on the porch, staring at Michelle's car, the lone car parked on the driveway.

'Sorry you had to witness all that drama with Lucas,' Emilia said. 'Old resentments, you know?'

'I get it.'

'When Alma went blind,' Emilia began, then stopped, unsure how to continue. She tried again, 'Something really awful happened.'

'You don't have to tell me if you don't want to,' Michelle said. 'You don't owe me an explanation.'

Emilia smiled, nodded. She wanted to tell Michelle that for months after it happened to Alma, Emilia would have auditory dreams, the kind of dreams experienced by people who had been blind since birth, as if in sleep she had slipped into a parallel world where she never had sight. It wasn't bad or disturbing for her—just different. She dreamt that she was roaming the streets. She could feel the sweat and grime on her skin, she could smell the days-old odour rising from her unwashed body, she could hear the jeepneys and the buses honking past, the angry drivers and pedestrians cursing at her as she barrelled past them, as she reached out her hands to them. She could feel the tremor in her windpipe, feel the muscle strain at the top of her eyelids as she tried to open her eyes as wide as she could. *I am blind!* She couldn't tell if it was a pronouncement of fear or relief. Her voice like someone else's voice. *I am blind! I am blind!*

Joaquin stepped out of the front door, now wearing a basketball cap.

'Heading off?' Emilia said.

'I'm going to see Sophie,' he said. 'Lucas is already there.'

He left the invitation unsaid, but he kept staring at her, lingering, waiting, bouncing on the balls of his feet.

'We need to go, though,' Emilia said.

Joaquin stopped bouncing. 'Are you sure?'

'Don't leave on my account, if you want to visit her,' Michelle said. 'There's no real rush.'

Emilia tried to scrape the mud off her shoes against one of the cement steps. She did come all this way, and she was never coming back. She knew this in her heart. She wanted her life here to feel so distant that the memories wouldn't hurt, that it would feel like another dull anecdote about someone else's life story being narrated to her on a car ride home.

'Well,' she said, 'I guess it wouldn't hurt to pop in for a quick hello.'

Joaquin's whispered *Yes!* and his subdued fist pump were so earnest that Emilia burst out laughing.

Michelle said she didn't mind staying back, but Emilia didn't want to leave her in a room full of desolate strangers. Sofia's house was only four streets away, and it had stopped raining, so Michelle could walk with them if she wanted to.

Michelle glanced at her car. 'Are you planning to come back here?'

Emilia wasn't sure if *here* meant Santa Clara or the wake, but her answer felt true for both. 'No,' she said.

'Then I should just drive you guys there.'

Emilia looked at Joaquin, who said to Michelle, 'If that's okay with you.'

'She can just park out front, and we can be on our way,' Emilia replied. To Michelle, she added: 'It won't take long, I promise.'

Joaquin climbed into the back seat, sitting in the middle. 'Nice car.'

'This old thing?' Michelle smiled, narrowly missing a flowerpot as she reversed out of the driveway. 'You should see my brother's car. That brat got the latest model, and he didn't even pay for it.'

A small silence, then Joaquin said, 'He didn't steal it, did he?' which made Michelle laugh.

'A gift from my gullible parents,' Michelle said, air-quoting. 'A "graduation gift". I didn't get a gift when I graduated!'

Joaquin and Emilia laughed, but they caught each other's eyes in the rear-view mirror, and they just let the silence settle and grow. She wondered what Michelle thought of Alma's home, with the rickety plastic chairs and the instant coffees and scuffed kitchen linoleum, she who came from peach curtains and maids and Papa's business trips and graduation gifts in the form of cars and the expectation of expensive flowers and a bowl of fruit on the table at every meal. Michelle's enthusiasm for instant coffee, looking around like a tourist, unperturbed by the grime because this grime was not hers, because she was just passing through. She thought of the small silence before Joaquin made his funny quip, wondered if Joaquin was thinking of the same thing she was thinking now: What a thing to do in an impoverished town, to casually complain about a good life.

Despite Michelle's generosity, Emilia still felt as if she had more to give, as if she were holding back something that Emilia was entitled to. It made her feel ugly.

She was glad when Michelle herself broke the silence. 'So how's Sofia? Lucas said she was sickly?'

'She has good days and bad days,' Joaquin said. 'She lives alone now, so Lucas and I visit every now and then.'

Emilia glanced at him through the rear-view mirror. 'She lives alone? Her father's dead?'

'Yes.' Joaquin said this with a quick tilt of his head, an impatient gesture, as though to say, *You should know this already.* 'Ten years ago, now.'

'I didn't know,' Emilia said, but then, why would she? 'I thought he was going to pull through.'

'She has no family here?' Michelle asked.

'Not in this province,' he said. 'And even if they lived nearby, I don't think they would want to—' He squirmed in his seat. 'It's hard to explain. Sophie's a nice person, but she's suffering. She's always in pain. Taking care of her can be challenging, you know.'

'But you do take care of her,' Michelle said. 'Wow. I wish I had friends like you. God bless you guys.'

Joaquin jumped out to open Sofia's gate. Her driveway was only large enough to fit one car. To Emilia, everything looked the same. There was the same dirty kitchen beyond the driveway, the same stack of soot-blackened iron pots and pans beneath the sink, the same washing machine that had turned from shiny grey to yellow in 1999, the same clothesline next to the mossy concrete wall, the same gigantic, yellow margarine tubs repurposed to collect rainwater.

The gate squeaked as Joaquin closed it. The front door was unlocked. He looked visibly upset by this. 'Sophie?'

The inside of Sophie's house looked as if she had started to pack up to move someplace else, and then decided against it halfway through the process. In the living room was a sofa, a small wooden table, and several large boxes, some of which were sealed with packaging tape and marked SOPHIE or BOOKS: LUCAS, scrawled on the side with a felt-tip pen. Emilia peeked in one of the boxes and saw old clothes, broken umbrellas, shoes with faux leather peeling in strips, empty perfume bottles, ancient-looking lotions and creams, spiral pads filled with notes. The ink fading into the pages stiff with age.

The only light source were the squares of weak sunlight streaming in through the open windows behind the sofa. Joaquin switched on the lights. The table was too low and too small for the space. It was probably pulled out from another room or from another living room set and was placed there just to have something to put things on. Beneath the table were mismatched plastic bowls, a pair of slippers, a pen cap.

'You'll have to forgive the mess,' Joaquin said, inviting them to sit on the sofa. 'Sophie's been trying to clear up some space for months now.'

They heard the whimpering when they were just about to sit down, followed by the sound of a door opening and Lucas' voice sailing in through the doorway. Emilia knew the doorway led to the kitchen, the dining area, and the bedrooms.

'Joaquin?' Lucas called out. 'Is that you?'

The whimpering was growing in intensity, rising in volume, turning into words: 'I don't—I don't want you to— just let me go—'

Lucas, tired, subdued, called back to Joaquin: 'I need a little help over here.'

The person—Sofia—was bawling now. Joaquin ran through the doorway. 'Oh, God,' Joaquin exclaimed, and then he was running back, holding a hand up. 'I'll be right back, okay? Just stay here.'

'Is she okay?' Michelle asked, but Joaquin was gone again.

'Stay here,' Emilia told her, and followed Joaquin deeper into the house. She followed the pained cries to the end of a dark corridor; the bathroom, a sliver of faint light slipping through a door left ajar, the light broken every now and then by shadows. An incoherent stream of words from Sofia, Joaquin murmuring to placate her, Lucas having none of it, a stern parent speaking to a stubborn child wailing in pain: 'You'll just keep bleeding if you don't stay put, is that what you want?'

'Hello?' Emilia said. The racket in the bathroom abruptly stopped as the corridor fell into a stunned silence. 'Sorry. I'm wondering if you need some help?'

Lucas' voice dropping to a whisper: 'She came with you?'

Sofia's tiny voice: 'Who's that?'

Emilia pushed the door wide open. At first, all she could see was the blood. Sofia was sitting on the bathroom floor, her back against the toilet, sweater the colour of a dusty rose pulled over a dress, left sweater arm pushed up as Lucas dabbed gauze on the deep, bleeding cuts on her forearm.

Joaquin was kneeling next to Sofia with his back towards the door. He glanced over his shoulder and sighed. 'I told you to stay in the living room, Lia.'

Sofia pushed against Lucas as she scrambled to get up, her open wounds pressing against his shirt front, swiping away the bloodied bandages he had balanced on one knee. 'Sophie!' he said in surprise.

Joaquin pitched forward to hold her by the elbow.

'Goddamn it,' Lucas mumbled, looking down at his blood-smeared shirt as the three of them rose from the floor.

Sofia paid no attention to either of them. She was staring at Emilia. Face wet with tears, eyes sunken, collarbones jutting out from the wide collar of her sweater, but overjoyed, Emilia realized with surprise and sorrow. Bleeding, in pain, but Sofia was overjoyed to see her.

'You came back,' Sofia said. Emilia didn't flinch as Sofia put her arms around her, soaking her in her blood, and instead leaned into Sofia's embrace. 'I knew you'd come back.'

'Our shirts got stained,' Emilia explained when she saw Michelle look up from her phone and frown. Both she and Lucas were now wearing baggy shirts with the words 'Santa Clara College'. Old gifts from Lucas, the first shirts Emilia could grab from Sofia's closet.

'Go, SCC,' Lucas said, carrying two chairs from the kitchen, an unlit cigarette sticking out of the corner of his mouth. Joaquin came in with another chair and helped Sofia sit down.

Sofia's arm was now properly bandaged and hidden by her sweater. Joaquin handed her a small red blanket, and Sofia draped it around herself.

'Can you—' Sofia said, pointing up.

'Sorry, girls,' Joaquin said, switching off the lights. 'Sophie likes it dark.'

Lucas pushed a chair towards Joaquin. 'Here you go, boss.'

'I just like the sunlight better,' Sofia said.

Lucas pointed out the window. 'That sunlight? It's overcast. You can't see anything in here. What?' The last word directed at Joaquin, who was glaring at him.

A quiet moment as they all settled in their seats. Emilia joined Michelle on the sofa. Sofia sat on the chair facing them, the weak light on her face. She was wearing dangling earrings, the red crystal beads catching the light. 'Sorry about all that,' Sofia said, looking at Michelle. 'I had a small accident.'

'As long as you're all right,' Michelle said. 'I like your earrings.'

Sofia touched her ear, smiled. 'Really? I made them myself.'

'You make your own jewellery? Cool.' Michelle looked around the silent room, as though waiting for something. Then continued, 'My name's Michelle, by the way.'

Emilia gasped, embarrassed. 'I'm so sorry, I completely forgot to introduce you—'

'This is Lia's friend from work,' Lucas said.

'I see,' Sofia said. 'Where do you work?'

Lucas sat back and lit his cigarette as Michelle began talking.

'I told you to stop smoking in here,' Sofia snapped at him, cutting Michelle off.

'I'll stop smoking if you stop cutting yourself.'

Sofia pulled the blanket tighter around her arms, as though she wanted to disappear into it.

'Did you do that to yourself, Sophie?' Emilia asked. She felt a twinge, an ache, a flash of memory. Alma in a dream. *I was trying to get to the muscle.*

'He's so rude,' Sofia said, talking to Michelle. 'Sorry about that. What were you saying?'

Michelle looked at Lucas, cocked an eyebrow. 'He is rude, isn't he,' she said. 'Good-looking, but so rude.'

Sofia stared at her in shock, and then she and Michelle were laughing together, suddenly allies, co-conspirators. Even Lucas had to chuckle. Emilia relaxed, stretching her legs, as Michelle began telling Sofia about their workplace, the wonky elevator in the building, her brother's annoying dog, her dreams of becoming a stockbroker, her last vacation in El Nido, her favourite places in Cebu—'My father's there now, actually'—jumping smoothly from one topic to another even when some of them were connected by the thinnest of threads. Sofia looked mesmerized, completely present, smiling and nodding at the right moments, the girl that Emilia remembered, leagues away from the bleeding woman she found crying on the bathroom floor just moments earlier.

Michelle was telling her about her coffee habit ('I can drink up to five cups a day, but I know I have to stop because I'm starting to get palpitations') when Sofia interrupted her.

'I didn't even offer you anything to drink,' she said. 'Where are my manners? Would you like some coffee?'

'Oh, it's okay,' Michelle said. 'We had coffee earlier at the—' She waved vaguely behind her, towards the road, towards the coffin surrounded by flowers in a stifling room four streets away. 'You know.'

'Where?' Sofia's face was open, expectant, smiling.

'Sophie,' Emilia said, as gently as she could. 'We were at Alma's.'

'Lia just came home for the wake,' Joaquin said. 'You know that, right?'

Sofia's smile faded, looking as if the wind had been knocked out of her. 'Oh.' She tucked stray wisps of hair behind her ear. 'Right. I knew that. I just forgot for a moment.'

She lifted the blanket up to her face and began to sob.

'I came here to see you too,' Emilia said, leaning forward, wanting to reach across the table to touch her hand.

'Bullshit,' Lucas said.

'Can you just,' Joaquin began to say, too exasperated to even finish the sentence.

Lucas looked mollified. 'I'll get Sophie some water.'

Sofia kept her face buried in the blanket until Lucas disappeared into the kitchen. She lifted her head, wiped her eyes, tried to fix her hair.

'So did you,' Sofia said, sniffling, 'did you take the bus to get here? The last bus to the city leaves at noon.' Out of reflex, Emilia glanced up at the clock on the wall above the door, a beige Seiko clock that must have been as old as the washing machine. It was now three in the afternoon.

'It's okay,' Michelle said. 'We drove here.'

'Are you kicking me out now, Sophie?' Emilia said, attempting a joke.

'No, stupid,' Sofia said.

They smiled at each other.

'We almost got lost on the way here, actually,' Michelle said. 'Then we came across this weird house.'

Lucas came back with a pitcher of ice water and some glasses on a plastic tray. 'A weird house, did you say?' He poured water into the glasses and handed them around, the ice cubes clinking, the glasses instantly sweating.

'Like a tiny house that I was sure was abandoned. Actually, it looked more like a toolshed. But there was a woman in it. She didn't say anything, though.'

'What did she look like?' Lucas was trying to come off looking blasé about it, but Emilia wasn't fooled.

'I didn't see her face. But,' Michelle held a finger up, 'she was wearing a veil.'

'A veil?' Joaquin said.

'A black veil, like the kind old ladies wear to church?' Michelle said, turning to Emilia. 'Right? Did you see that?'

Emilia could see Lucas, Joaquin, and Sofia staring at her. Waiting.

'I don't know,' Emilia said.

Michelle shrugged. 'Maybe my eyes were playing tricks on me. But you were spooked. You dragged me away from there.' She bent down to tighten the laces on her shoes. 'I can't blame you. It was a bit spooky, even in broad daylight.'

'She dragged you away?' Lucas said. He crossed his arms. 'Did you come across it by accident? Or did Lia tell you where to turn?'

'The GPS was acting up,' Michelle said. 'Although Emilia did tell me where to turn at some point.' She looked intrigued, amused. 'Why?'

'It sounds like one of those houses we believed were haunted when we were kids,' Joaquin said.

Such horrible actors. Emilia turned to Sofia to see how she was reacting to all this. Sofia was wide-eyed with fury and fear. She sprang from her seat and stepped behind the sofa, closing the windows with a bang. Now the room was pitch-black, the lit cigarette between Lucas' fingers the only point of illumination. Sofia sat back down and covered her ears with her hands.

Joaquin and Lucas shared a worried glance.

Sofia rocked back and forth in her seat.

Emilia and Michelle moved closer together, Emilia's left knee knocking against Michelle's right. 'Should we open the windows?' Emilia asked, even though she knew that even if Sofia said yes, she would be too frightened to do so.

Sofia sat up, fixing her blanket with trembling hands, using it to cover her head. In the darkness, she looked as if she were wearing a veil. 'A few years ago, I came across this concept called "moral luck",' she said. 'I've been thinking about it ever since. Living in this town, in this house, that's all you can do, really, to fill the hours. Think. Do you know the concept?'

Emilia and Michelle glanced at each other. Sofia's thoughts didn't just jump, they somersaulted.

They shook their heads.

'Sophie,' Lucas said. 'Don't be ridiculous. It's too dark—'

'We tend to think that our moral standing is unwavering, that it remains the same in any context,' Sofia said, ignoring him. 'But moral luck asks, can we really be praised or blamed for our actions if they are caused by circumstances beyond our control? Let's say a man is standing in line and a woman bumps into his back. The man would be quick to blame her, to judge her as a person who has complete disregard about a fellow human's well-being. But what if the man finds out that the woman was just pushed by the person behind her? The man doesn't blame her then, because he now knows her resulting action was caused by something beyond her control.

'And yet, how would you feel towards the woman if she not only bumped into the man but accidentally pushed him in front of a speeding bus? What if she accidentally pushed him, but there was no speeding bus, and the man just fell on the asphalt and scraped his elbow? Isn't it ridiculous that a speeding bus could spell the difference between a life of moral judgment and suffering, and a few minutes of apologizing to an angry fellow commuter?

'Let's say you lived in a town hit by a terrible storm, and the next day you break into your neighbour's house to steal food because you are starving. Now you are a thief.

If you had lived in another town, in a town not hit by the storm, you would still be leading a good life, a life where you are not a thief. Everything we do depends so much on circumstances and opportunities we cannot change. So, do we even have control on our lives? Can we be considered morally responsible if there are factors beyond our power? Are we good, or are we just lucky?'

Lucas stood up with a sigh to open the windows. The light showed tears streaming down Sofia's face.

'You're spending too much time with Philosopher Lucas and his books,' Joaquin said.

'It's scary to think about,' Sofia said, ignoring him too. Ignoring all of them, as though she were confessing her sins to an unseen force. The blanket fell to her waist, and Emilia could see her rubbing her hands up and down her arms, lifting up her sleeves, revealing her bandaged left forearm, her right forearm pink with scars left behind by wounds shaped like jagged squares. 'Who would I have been, if I had not been born here, if I did not meet the people I have met? Is my life even my life?'

For a moment, Emilia could not speak. She stood up and knelt by Sofia's chair. She cleared her throat, gestured towards Sofia's arms, keeping her voice soft so only Sofia could hear. 'Why would you cut yourself up like this?' Asking the question even though she already knew the answer. Even though Alma had already told her the answer.

Sofia matched her voice, whispered her responses. 'To look like her,' she said. 'So she can see that I'm worthy. That I'm giving her something precious to me.'

Emilia touched her knee. 'Why?'

'She won't let me sleep. We didn't finish it. It's been twelve years.'

We didn't finish it. It was like an accusation.

No.

Emilia stood up suddenly, as if she had been touched by flame.

'I think we're leaving now,' she said.

One afternoon, Emilia saw Pauline leading a black goat across an empty field. Or, at least, what she thought was an empty field. This was a month after Mia was laid to rest. Days prior, Pauline's father had a second heart attack. Similar to what happened after the first one, he was rushed to the local hospital and given medication. This time, however, he was being urged to have bypass surgery at the Philippine Heart Center in the city, which had better equipment and more experienced specialists. The doctors had recommended it the first time, but Pauline's family could not afford it. Now the doctors were making it clear that a second heart attack was often life-threatening. If Pauline's father didn't undergo the surgery, he might end up dead.

Emilia and her friends had heard their own parents talking. They compared their stories. Their parents said that the last time they visited Pauline's father, he screamed that they should just let him die, because what was the point? What was the point of all this?

They were thinking of asking the school if they could hold a town fundraiser for Pauline's family at the gym, maybe even write the mayor's office and ask for help. Emilia was on her way to Pauline's home to share all these ideas when she spotted her walking down an unpaved road into the field, leading a goat on a bright red leash.

Pauline's family reared two goats and a few chickens on their property. She had mentioned before that her father's dream was to buy a farm in Bukidnon, his hometown, and retire there with his wife, happily raising goats and chickens and carabaos while their daughters began their exciting lives in the city. But now his eldest was dead and his wife was contemplating selling their land to pay for his surgery, a surgery he was refusing to undergo because he wanted to die. Pauline still went to school at her mother's insistence and filled out college applications, but even when she sat with her friends in class or in the cafeteria, she seemed very far away, her reactions slow and inconsistent, as though she were listening in on their conversations from deep underwater.

Emilia didn't call out when she saw Pauline, and instead walked into the tall grass, following at a distance. She was thinking her friend probably took the goat here to graze, but why here, and why so late? The field looked golden in the light, which was quickly fading, the sky a deep orange, flat and cloudless.

She stopped dead when she saw the house. It appeared so suddenly, as though it were an animal that had crept up on her in complete silence.

It was a small house, no bigger than the toolshed in school where they first met Lucas. Pauline was leading the goat towards the house when the goat began bleating, stamping her feet, pulling away on her leash. Pauline whipped her head around, and Emilia dropped to her haunches. Seeing that the goat was attempting to escape, Pauline pulled harder on the leash. 'Come on!' she screamed. 'Come on, stop it!' Emilia watched this tug-of-war through blades of grass. It didn't last long. After a minute, Pauline dropped to her knees, wailing like a small child. The goat moved closer to lick her cheeks, ears perking up, friendly again. Pauline put her arms around her and buried her face in the goat's neck.

Emilia stayed down, listening to Pauline's muffled cries. She didn't even cry like this during her sister's funeral. In his sermon, the priest said that grief came in waves, and perhaps this was the crest of a wave Pauline didn't even foresee was coming.

The goat seemed to have seen Emilia hiding in the grass. She bleated towards her direction, a small cry, playful, not like the scream she was making upon seeing the house. Emilia kept herself as still as she possibly could, until Pauline stood up, wiped her face with her shirt sleeve, and walked back home with the goat.

Emilia stayed in the grass for a few more moments. It was dark now, the golden light receding from the house, door open like a mouth. She stood up and ran across the field towards the road, towards what felt like safety. She still didn't understand what happened just then, until a few days later, when they were all sitting in Pauline's backyard, keeping her company as they hashed out the details of the fundraiser, and Sofia looked around and said, 'Where's your other goat? The black one?'

'Stolen, probably, I don't know,' Pauline muttered under her breath, and Emilia thought, *She tried again.*

'Aw,' Sofia said. 'Wasn't that your favourite?'

She tried again, and the goat entered the house this time.

They couldn't get a town fundraiser off the ground. Everyone was struggling, and whoever was in the mayor's office wouldn't even pick up the phone. They scaled down

the idea and got permission from Miss Cardenas, their
class adviser, to instead hold a bazaar at the school. 'But
only within your year level,' she said, looking sad herself to
bring this news from upper management. They liked Miss
Cardenas. When Pauline's father was taken to the hospital,
she was the only teacher who dropped by to check on her
and her family. She was cool and funny, and at least twenty
years younger than the median age of teachers in their
school, but she was too low on the totem pole to exert any
real influence on their behalf.

They were given one Saturday to use the biggest classroom
in the school as the location of the bazaar, where they could
sell home-cooked meals, clothes, shoes, old furniture, second-
hand books, anything they could think of, with proceeds
going to Pauline's family. Lucas promised he would talk to his
classmates at the private school about sending goods to sell
or even giving money to add to the donation funds.

'Cold, hard cash,' Emilia said. 'That's the way to go.' She
was in Lucas' room, helping him pack the books they would
bring to the bazaar. Lucas made a show of keeping the door
open so his mother wouldn't have conniptions.

His father had started clearing his home office—*so fancy,*
Emilia had teased—and put aside stationery for them to
decorate signage and for admin tasks. Pens, paper, markers,
highlighters, clipboards, sticky notes, rolls of manila paper.
Emilia started packing them, using one of the markers to
write BAZAAR SIGNS on top of the box.

'You have no idea what cheapskates these private school
kids are,' Lucas said.

'I think I do,' she said. 'You're one of them.'

Lucas laughed.

She couldn't tell if the floor of his bedroom was covered with vinyl or actual floorboards, but she had always liked how shiny it looked, how it reflected the sunlight coming in through the windows behind his headboard. On his shelves were an entire set of encyclopaedias, a copy of *The Divine Comedy*, *Don Quixote of the Mancha*, an Atlas, *The Kingfisher Children's Bible*, and several pocket Bibles bound in faux blue leather. There were several philosophy books: *Beyond Good and Evil*, *The Republic*, *Meditations*, *Critique of Pure Reason*. How clean and tidy everything was in his uncluttered, elegant life. His father was but a humble teacher, sure, but Emilia knew his parents also ran a lucrative business in the city, some wholesale operation that would fall apart after everything else fell apart, his mother falling ill, trapping Lucas here when he could have gone anywhere. If only he knew. But they didn't know. None of it had happened yet.

So Emilia asked a question with an excitement that was now just painful, in hindsight. 'What universities did you apply to? UP, of course. I think we all applied to UP.'

'I applied to all of them.'

'Even SCC?' Emilia scoffed. 'Your mother would never.'

'It was just for safety,' he said. 'Why does everyone react that way?'

'Your mother wants you to go to UST,' she said. 'You know, the good Catholic school, away from the crazy Jesuits. So you can be a proper god-fearing doctor. I don't think you should apply to Ateneo even. It'll break her heart.'

'Did you apply to Ateneo?'

'We can never afford it.'

'But didn't you apply to UST too? That university's also expensive.'

'Not as expensive.'

'There are scholarships, you know,' he said, sealing a box with masking tape. 'It won't hurt to try.'

'I guess.'

Emilia would think about this moment sometimes, she and Lucas sitting on the cool floorboards, covered in book dust.

'Wouldn't it be great if we all got accepted to the same university and we rented a whole house near campus?' She glanced at the open door. 'Oh, but your mother won't like that. I think she'll drop you off at the male-only campus residence. Away from temptation.'

How fun it was to dream about the future, to see each university as a new pathway.

'Good God,' he said with a disgusted groan, which made her laugh.

Remember? Remember how fun it all was?

'Was that all of it?' Emilia asked. They stood up at the same time. 'I think all of the books have been packed.'

'Pauline got a good head start, I guess,' he said.

'Pauline?'

'She was here yesterday. Didn't I tell you?'

He gently kicked at something under his bed. Emilia looked down and felt her heart jump to her throat. At first, she thought it was a person stuffed in an empty sack of rice, but looking closer, she saw the top of the head, the peeling paint, the white skull made of plastic and rubber.

It was one of the life-size human anatomical models from his father's home office.

'Father was thinking of donating this to the school,' he said, 'but Pauline wanted it.'

'Pauline wanted this?' she said. 'What for?'

He shrugged. 'I just cleaned it up for her.' He pulled out the sack. He had bent the mannequin's legs so it would fit, tied plastic strings at either end of the sack to serve as a strap so it could be carried like luggage.

Emilia lifted it up. It was a bit heavy, but easy enough to carry on your shoulder. Like a bag of the strangest-looking groceries.

'This is very weird,' Emilia said.

'I just didn't ask why,' he said. 'She seemed off lately.' He turned to her. 'Are you headed that way? I can pay for the tricycle.'

Pauline was feeding the chickens when Emilia arrived with the sack.

'Oh, good,' she said, wiping feed off her hands on the back of her shorts as Emilia approached. 'You brought it. Thank you.'

Emilia handed the sack over. 'What's going on with you?' she said. 'Why do you need this?'

But Pauline was in a hurry. She hugged the package close to her chest and strode past the chickens, making them cluck and scatter away in a cloud of dust. 'Come back in an hour,' she said over her shoulder. 'Where you found me with the goat.'

Emilia felt cold all over. 'What?'

'It told me you where there.' Pauline stopped by the door. The chickens had calmed down and had returned to their food, pecking at the grains on the ground. It was nearing dusk, and the chickens were having their fill before they settled to roost. 'I didn't see you, but it said you were watching.'

'Who said?' Emilia demanded. 'Who said I was watching?'

'Thank you for not telling everyone what I did,' Pauline said, entering the house. 'See you soon.'

For the next hour, Emilia debated with herself whether she should tell the others. But she didn't want to embarrass Pauline. In the end, she went on her own. The only witness.

'Someone lives in this house,' Pauline said. In her hands was a piece of black tulle. It was evening now, the field leached of all light save for a flickering white glow within the house.

'Who'd want to live here?'

'A god lives in this house.'

'God lives in this house?'

'*A* god.'

Later they stepped inside, and Emilia found that the glow was coming from a portable lamp Pauline had set on the floor.

There was no furniture, save for a lone chair in the centre of the room. She couldn't see any hallways or doors leading to other rooms.

They stood near the front door, and Pauline gestured to the chair. It took Emilia a moment before she could make sense of what she was seeing.

Seated on the chair was the life-size human anatomical model, the mannequin Pauline had borrowed from Lucas. Half of its face had no skin, the better to reveal the brain, the skull, the circular white eyeball, the vessels, the muscles; its torso cracked open to display the organs, the red-and-blue-veined heart between the lungs, the chocolate-brown liver, the beige intestines. Right now, Emilia could see the organs through a layer of sheer fabric. Pauline had dressed the mannequin in a white chiffon gown.

'I used one of my sister's old dresses,' Pauline explained, approaching the mannequin and opening her arms to unroll the black tulle. She placed the fabric over the mannequin, a veil that covered it from head to foot. A grotesque bride. She leaned forward until she was nose-to-nose with it. She stayed in this pose for what felt to Emilia like an eternity.

Finally, Pauline straightened her back, glanced over her shoulder. She was smiling. 'Isn't it perfect?'

It was obscene.

What was this supposed to be? An altar?

Emilia wanted to run away.

'First, you need to give it something that is precious to you,' Pauline said. 'Precious doesn't mean expensive. That was my mistake at first. Did you know I tried to give it one of my mother's necklaces? I was thinking, this should be enough, surely.'

'Pau,' Emilia said, whispering, as though she were afraid the mannequin would hear, 'I want to go.'

'Sit down on the floor, Lia.'

'But—'

'Then,' Pauline said, speaking over her, 'it needed a shelter, a doorway. It needed a shelter because you'd go blind if you saw it with your naked eyes. I didn't know what I could use,' she waved at the veiled mannequin seated in its chair, 'but I had the idea when I was at Lucas' yesterday and saw his father taking this out of his office.'

Pauline had gone insane. What else could explain this?

'If it found your first offering acceptable,' she continued, 'it would walk through the doorway and inhabit the house you created.'

'Do you want me to call your mother?' Emilia asked.

'Just sit down,' Pauline said. 'Sit down and be ready for a life of good fortune.'

'What?'

Pauline took out a piece of white chalk from her pocket and drew a ragged circle around the mannequin's chair.

'It can't bring my sister back,' Pauline said, drawing symbols inside the circle as she spoke, like a math teacher explaining the equations she was writing on a chalkboard. But the symbols Pauline was drawing were completely foreign to Emilia. 'It can't kill the man who hit her. It can't turn back time. I already asked. But that's all right. We move forward.'

Grief came in waves. Was that what was happening here? 'You know, Pau,' Emilia said, gently, 'let's just take a breath and get out of here. You've been through a lot.'

Pauline suddenly laughed. 'You think a bazaar will solve all of this?'

This statement hit Emilia like a punch in the face.

'You wanted this, didn't you,' Pauline said, slapping the chalk dust from her hand.

Emilia frowned. 'I don't even know what *this* is,' she said. 'I don't even know what's happening here.'

'Why did you follow me that day?' Pauline replied. 'Why didn't you tell anyone what you saw?'

'I don't know,' Emilia said. 'What would I even say? That you killed your own goat? For what?' She glanced at the abomination in front of her, the veiled form, the writing on the floor. She felt a howl of despair rise from within her: 'What are you even *doing*?'

'You're a part of this now,' Pauline said. Then, more firmly: 'Sit. Down.'

Pauline herself didn't sit down. She knelt. She pulled Emilia down with her. Emilia, surprised, crashed to the floor with a yelp and found herself on her knees in front of the veiled form, lit from behind by Pauline's white lamp.

'Pau, stop it.'

One.

Emilia looked over at Pauline, who was staring hard at the mannequin.

'Come on,' Emilia said, tugging at Pauline's arm.

Two.

'Let's just go. Please?'

Pauline looked unsure. Nothing was happening.

What were they even waiting for?

Three.

'You've been through a lot,' Emilia said.

Four.

'I understand that, and I'm sorry, but Pau, you're really scaring me. Can we just—'

Five.

A gasp of terror from Pauline.

The sound of someone taking a deep, hungry breath.

Emilia turned her head to look.

The mannequin was breathing.

The mannequin was alive.

Emilia saw the concave shape of the black veil over the mannequin's rubber mouth, and felt as if she were being submerged underwater, her lungs filling with ice. Sweat broke out all over her body, making her feel colder than she already was.

Pauline's hand shot out and gripped her wrist. At first, she thought it was to give her comfort. Later, she realized it was to keep her in place.

The mannequin jerked its head and limbs like an epileptic. This went on for another torturous minute, Emilia's head filled with only one thought: *This can't be happening this can't be happening this can't be happening this can't be happening—*

She could feel Pauline sweating from her palm wrapped around her wrist.

Another deep breath, and the mannequin relaxed on the chair, folded its hands on its lap, leaned forward. Tilted its head like a person finally ready to listen.

Pauline was crying. 'You believe me now,' she said. A statement. Not a question. Pauline's hand was still gripping her wrist.

Emilia jerked away with all her might and burst out of the house, running through the grass, up the road. She could hear someone breathing behind her, giving chase. Was it Pauline, or was it whatever it was that resided within that mannequin now? Emilia didn't know, she didn't want to look back. She kept running and running until she was back in the town square, surrounded by lights and the gong of church bells and people staring at her as she bent over and threw up on the sidewalk.

She limped back home, shivering and crying, and locked herself in her room before her parents could see her. She said she was not feeling well when they called her for dinner.

Pauline was not in school the next day. She continued to miss classes for a week. They thought her father had taken a turn for the worse, but the next Monday, they heard from their teachers that Pauline's father had been transferred to the Heart Center and was recovering well from surgery.

Miss Cardenas did not report to work for several days. The admin office said she had filed vacation leave to visit her parents in Bicol, but that wasn't for another week. People just assumed she quit without telling anyone.

That was September. They never saw Pauline again in school. They heard that she had an arrangement with the high school to continue studying, so she could graduate on time and still help her mother take care of her father in the city.

The school called Miss Cardenas' parents in Naga City to check if she had gone home. She had not. She was not in the house she was renting in Santa Clara, which still had all her belongings, save for the shoulder bag she usually brought with her to the school. The bag contained almost everything she needed to live her life: house keys, phone, wallet with some cash, all her IDs and credit cards. Eventually, the police got involved, but whatever development happened with her case got lost in the noise. It was a mere ripple in a sea of disappearances. The town gossip mill got more traction, despite the disparate narratives: Miss Cardenas ran off with a lover, she was hiding from debtors, she got pregnant, she found a job abroad.

How could Emilia even begin to explain what she had seen? Perhaps Pauline didn't either, perhaps that was why she made her stay, so Emilia could see it with her own eyes, so Pauline didn't have to reduce the experience to mere words.

Emilia never told anyone. Her friends asked if she was just worried about the upcoming release of university results, and she let them believe that, rather than tell them that she had experienced the universe tilt on its axis.

Months passed. Before long, what she witnessed felt more and more like a dream.

University results started coming out in December. Christmas came, then the new year. The University of the Philippines, their top choice, was always the last to release results. In February, Emilia checked the university website, and there was Pauline's name, in black and white, on the list of students who were successfully granted admission to the flagship campus in Quezon City.

Emilia dreamt of Pauline that night. They were back inside the house, kneeling in front of a dark form completely covered by a black veil.

'Maybe I'll see you on campus,' Emilia said.

Pauline didn't even turn to look at her. 'You will never see me again,' she said.

Emilia didn't want to look at the form sitting on the chair in front of them, so she kept staring at Pauline's profile. 'I don't want to be a part of this. It's—'

What word was she looking for? Evil? Demonic? Wrong?

'You're a part of this now,' Pauline said. 'Whether you choose to or not.'

She felt goosebumps move up her arms. 'What happened after I ran away?' Dread weighed on her like a foot slowly pressing her face to the floor. 'What did you do?'

Pauline looked straight ahead, her expression peaceful. 'You'll see.'

The car would not start.

Michelle turned the key to the Start position and nothing happened. The instrument panel remained dark. She could not turn on the headlights. She tried jiggling the key in the ignition, tried moving the transmission from Park to Neutral before turning the key, but the engine stayed dead.

It had started to rain again, rain drops plinking on the roof, on the yellow margarine tubs in Sofia's dirty kitchen. Michelle lifted the hood up with Emilia standing next to her. The others stood on the porch, Sofia hugging herself, Joaquin with his hands in his pockets, Lucas lighting up another cigarette.

'Do you think it's the battery?' he asked, blowing smoke out the side of his mouth.

'Shit,' Michelle said, talking to herself. 'It could be. I can't turn on the headlights.'

'Do you have jumper cables?' Emilia asked.

'No. But even if I did, it's not like there's another car around.' Michelle called out to the peanut gallery. 'Would you know if there's a car repair shop nearby?'

'You'd have to go to Paombong or Malolos,' Joaquin said. 'There's a mechanic from the next town that my father knew. I can give him a call, but his shop is very busy. I doubt he'd be here before morning.'

Michelle lowered the hood, cursing under her breath.

'We can just take the bus,' Emilia said, at the same time remembering what Sofia had said earlier. *The last bus to the city leaves at noon.*

The look on Michelle's face said that she remembered this too. 'I wouldn't want to leave the car here, anyway,' she said. 'If I can help it.'

'You know you can stay over,' Sofia said, moving close to the edge of the porch, rainwater drenching her toes. 'I have an extra room. The mechanic can be here in the morning.'

Emilia turned back to Michelle, ignoring this suggestion. 'Do you think your brother can pick us up?'

'I guess.' Michelle sighed, taking out her phone. 'My mother's going to kill me.'

The rain started coming down harder, sounding like gravel being poured on the rooftop. Emilia couldn't even see past the gate, the sheets of water obscuring her view. They all walked back into the house.

Joaquin called the mechanic, who, in addition to being busy, now wouldn't want to leave his shop, given the weather. Same with Michelle's brother.

'I wouldn't expect him to do me a favour on a perfect sunny day,' she said, 'but he's in the city right now with his friends, and apparently there was a big pile-up on NLEX and nothing is moving.' She glanced at her phone, reading a news update. '"An approximate eight-kilometre build-up from the site of the crash."'

'Jesus,' Emilia said.

They were alone in the living room. Everyone else had dispersed to get the guest room ready, to look around in the kitchen to see if there was enough food for dinner, to see if the ceiling was going to cave in from the sheer force of the rain.

'So, he'll just stay in the city,' Michelle said. 'He's planning to pick up my father at the airport tomorrow before heading back.'

'I'm really sorry about this.'

Michelle shrugged. 'It's not your fault. *I'm* sorry, honestly. That stupid car. Now it looks like we're going to be stuck here for the night.'

If Michelle didn't insist on driving her, she would have just taken the bus, kept her eye on the clock, left the wake after an hour, caught the last bus out of here. She would already be in her high-rise, condo-share apartment, watching the rain from a great height, waiting for another week to begin.

If Alma didn't die—

If Sofia didn't see the house—

If Pauline didn't meet whoever was residing there—

If Mia didn't succumb to her wounds—

If the police didn't use violence—

If the world was just and kind—

'Looking on the bright side,' Michelle said, 'this is way better than being stuck in eight-kilometre traffic.'

They saw Joaquin on their way to the kitchen, entering the guest room with an armful of bedsheets and pillows. In the kitchen, Lucas was washing a pot. Only the light over the stove had been switched on. Sofia was sitting at the kitchen table, in darkness, watching him.

'I figure I should start making rice,' he explained as they entered.

Sofia turned to them. 'You're staying?'

The rain hitting the roof was so loud Emilia had to speak a little louder to even hear herself. 'We'll be out of here first thing in the morning.'

'Thank you so much, by the way,' Michelle gushed. 'We'll be out of your hair soon, don't worry.'

Sofia didn't smile, didn't react, but her eyes were curious, alive, as she held Emilia's gaze. She looked like a little child brimming with excitement and working hard at concealing this excitement. She rested her arms on the table, clenching and unclenching her fists.

Michelle looked in the refrigerator and took out beef, bell peppers, potatoes, carrots, a bag of green peas. She added this to the cloves of garlic and onion that Lucas had already taken out of the cupboard and placed on the kitchen counter.

'Can we make something with these?' she asked.

Lucas nodded. 'If we add liver spread, tomato sauce, and bay leaves we can make caldereta.'

'Really?' Michelle said, pleased with herself. 'And to think I just grabbed whatever looked edible in the refrigerator.'

'What?' Emilia laughed. She couldn't help herself. 'I thought you knew what you were doing!'

'I don't know how to cook,' Michelle said.

'You've got personal chefs doing that for you?' Lucas said, opening the cupboards.

'Oh, sure,' Michelle said. 'They go by the name of Shopwise and 7-Eleven.'

Joaquin entered the kitchen at this point, glanced at the ingredients on the counter, at the cans of tomato sauce and liver spread in Lucas' arms, and said, 'Looks like caldereta for dinner,' sending Emilia and Michelle into another bout of laughter.

'What did I miss?' he asked Lucas, puzzled.

Emilia switched on all the lights. The kitchen was too dark without sunlight, and she found it demented to work with knives in darkness. The fluorescent lights buzzed like wasps before blinking on. Sofia didn't protest. Emilia watched her as they prepared dinner, as she listened to Joaquin gently tell Michelle which vegetables to cut and how to cut them. Less than an hour ago, Sofia was bawling and bleeding on the bathroom floor, going on and on about moral luck. What was she thinking now?

As they cooked, Sofia sat with a far-off gaze, but would snap to attention and answer whenever Michelle murmured a question. ('What are you looking for? A can opener? There's a can opener in that drawer. No, not that one. *There.*') She stood up at the end of the hour, as if the stove dial that Lucas turned was also the knob that switched her on. Joaquin told her to sit down but she wanted to do it, 'Just let me do this, please.' She took out the plates and cutlery from the cupboards and proceeded to set the table: glass, plate, spoon, fork, glass, plate, spoon, fork, glass, plate, spoon, fork. Lucas and Joaquin set down the bowl of rice and a bowl of steaming hot caldereta.

Sofia surveyed the table wordlessly, as though they had laid a feast and she were overwhelmed with choices.

'I can't believe I actually cooked something,' Michelle said, clapping her hands.

'Thank you so much for this,' Sofia said, and Emilia was struck by the emotion in her voice. 'Isn't this nice, Lia? Just like old times.'

What old times? Emilia could hardly enjoy the caldereta. The food itself turned out pretty tasty, but every tiny movement from Sofia made her want to sit up and brace herself.

The rain fell hard again while they were eating, making the lights flicker. A buzz of a mobile phone, followed by Joaquin walking out of the kitchen and coming back with a pill box marked with the days of the week. Sofia opened the tiny window marked *Saturday* and took out five multicoloured pills and downed them all at once with water.

They heard a soft *plip* of a raindrop falling on the floor, which continued, becoming louder. There was a hole in the kitchen ceiling. Sofia glanced at the dripping ceiling and said, 'It's okay,' even though Emilia could see the tense cords of muscles in her neck.

'Should I get a bucket?' Lucas asked.

Sofia shook her head no. 'Just keep eating, it's fine.'

'We need to get your roof looked at sooner or later,' Joaquin said. 'I think there's also a leak in the bathroom.'

No word from Sofia as she nibbled on a cut of meat she seemed to have been nibbling on for the past twenty minutes.

Small, aimless chatter between Joaquin and Michelle about cooking, about the best cuts of meat to use depending on the recipe, about how good this caldereta is—'Isn't it amazing, I'm surprised myself'—but other than that, the table was silent. Emilia was too tired to jump in, but she could see that Michelle was uneasy with the silence and looking for a way to fold Sofia into the conversation.

'So just like old times?' Michelle said to Sofia. 'You used to do this a lot? Cook together, have dinner?'

Sofia drank from her glass of water, slowly. She smacked her lips, arranged her utensils on her plate. 'Before I met them,' she said, 'I didn't have any friends. And they're an odd bunch, aren't they? Take Lucas.' A hint of a sly smile. 'He'd say things like, "According to Sartre, existence is problematic." Who talks like that?'

Lucas laugh-coughed into a fist.

'We're an odd bunch, especially in a town like this.'

Sofia's smile was so brilliant, so unexpected, that it drowned out every other sound. Michelle placed her elbow on the table, leaned closer.

'We told each other stories,' Sofia said. 'We'd walk each other to and from school and tell stories.'

Her smile disappeared and the dripping ceiling assaulted them like a ticking time bomb. *Plip. Plip. Plip.*

'There was a girl taking a walk one morning,' she said, 'and she found an empty house in a field. But the house wasn't empty. Whoever lived in the house wanted a gift, a shelter—'

'Sophie,' Emilia said. A warning, a challenge. She looked around the table. Lucas and Joaquin stared back at her.

'A story can be magic, conjured from nothing,' Sofia continued, 'or an excavation, just a process of uncovering what is already there. What if I were uncovering something that was already there?'

She continued nibbling on the piece of meat at the end of her fork.

'Sorry.' Michelle sat up and reached for more caldereta. 'I don't get it.'

Emilia shook her head at her: *Don't worry about it.*

To Sofia, she said, softly, 'Have you ever heard of *folie à deux*?'

Sofia shook her head, the meat still in her mouth. An unsettling image. '*Folie à plusieurs*,' she said, her voice muffled by the bite.

Part II

Folie À Plusieurs

If Emilia were to tell a story about Sofia, it would be this:

Sofia no longer remembered her mother, who died when she was young. Her father never remarried. He worked as an electrician in a neighbouring town, and Sofia could go for days without seeing him, even though they lived in the same house.

She often wondered out loud what her life would have been like if her mother had stayed alive. She wondered if she would be less lonely. She must have been a happy child because her aunts and uncles always said so whenever they visited, but she listened to these stories as if they were reminiscing about a child who had already died.

At least she met friends easily in high school, but she had a difficult time following her lessons, which didn't impress her father.

He was a hard man who measured his worth based not on gentleness and sympathy, but on how well he provided for his small family. His daughter ate three times a day and had a roof over her head; therefore, he was a good man. He saw demotivation as simply the excuse of the lazy, or the unintelligent. He would often make remarks like, 'You want to study in an expensive university in the city, but you can't even pass your high school exams,' or 'Keep it up and you'll amount to nothing.'

Despite Sofia's fervent wish to prove him wrong, her father's cruel prophecy came true: She didn't pass the entrance exam to UP, her choice university, while all her friends did. (Emilia, who once raised the idea of renting a whole house near campus, just for the five of them, stopped talking about it.) UP was also one of the few universities in the city that they could afford. At that point, Sofia's father seemed to lose interest in her, like a dog who had chewed a plastic toy to the core. 'Do whatever you want, but you can no longer ask money from me,' he said, and so they continued their complicated dance around the house to avoid each other.

Sofia, likewise, lost interest in herself.

After the holidays, she found part-time employment as an admin assistant at the local health clinic. On the news now almost every night was coverage of protests in the city, of university students going missing, but she couldn't focus on these stories. They were just another item on the long list of things that made her feel helpless. Instead, she spent her time at home watching bootleg copies of American films and TV shows. She watched YouTube videos about making bead earrings, and started making costume jewellery by hand, which some of the patients at the clinic bought from her for fifty pesos apiece.

Every first of the month, she would put a few bills on top of the TV with a small note: 'Tatay, for the utilities and groceries.' A gesture he never refused, but also never acknowledged.

One day she learned that an older cousin now worked in Quezon City, and Sofia started texting her, asking her about her time in UP.

One day, Sofia would think, she'd deposit her savings at the rural bank in town. One day.

But most days she felt as if she were half-asleep. She couldn't see past the clipboards and papers at the clinic, couldn't see past the newscaster saying their town's name on the news, couldn't imagine her life becoming better, or worse. All she could see was a straight, unwavering line, her body hunched over a table, bending wires to create earrings until the end of the world.

In an alternative life, what could Sofia have done differently to escape this narrative?

She could have packed her belongings and hopped on a bus to the city, leaving a short note for her father, knowing there was no other way to move forward except to go to a place where nobody knew her and her past failures.

In Quezon City, she could have stayed with her cousin, and spent a year working in fast-food restaurants and studying for the university entrance exams for the next intake year. Away from the pressures of her high school, of her father, of an imagined deadline for certain successes in life, she would have realized she wasn't as dim-witted as she believed. She could have passed the UPCAT and chose Communication Arts as a major, and continued making jewellery on the side. She could have signed up for the university theatre as a production assistant. She could have made props for plays and festivals, sold her handmade jewellery at the campus' yearly Christmas bazaar, interned at the University Chancellor's office, made friends.

She could have sent her father a text one summer, updating him about her life. His reply would be brief, and cruel. Something like: *What kind of job will you even get with a major like that?* She could have realized it was normal—necessary— to shed people, and that her father's happiness was not her responsibility. She could have received an appointment in the Chancellor's office as a member of the permanent staff after graduation. She could have celebrated the end of her studies with her friends from Santa Clara, who had all graduated a year earlier than her, but who cares? What was a year?

Maybe, while drinking with her colleagues after work, in Quezon City, or maybe even by the ocean in a foreign country, she would remember the Sofia sitting at her table in her room in Santa Clara. That Sofia thought her life was hopeless, thought her sadness was a wall she could not scale.

But here she was, on the other side of the wall.

None of it happened.

In this life, Sofia took a walk one morning, and saw the house.

In the neck are the left and right internal and external carotid arteries, located on either side. The external carotid artery brings blood to the scalp, face, and neck, while the internal carotid artery supplies blood to the brain. A puncture wound to the neck can cause airway occlusion or haemorrhagic shock from blood loss.

They found Miss Cardenas' body in late February, hastily buried in an empty plot of land near the edge of town, unseen and undisturbed for months until the owner and his carpenter did a site visit after the holidays and caught a whiff of something rotting. Miss Cardenas had two stab wounds in her neck. When the knife first went in, it did not stab any major artery or vessel. It hit the internal carotid artery the second time.

When they first heard the news, the questions her friends asked, to Emilia's ears, sounded naïve and idiotic. *How could anyone do this? How could anyone hate her?* Questions a child would ask.

All she could think about was Pauline hugging her beloved goat after failing to lure it into the house, Miss Cardenas' attacker trying a second time for that fatal blow as her victim lifted her hands to her throat, the blood gushing out of her mouth and out of the wound in pulses, cool and young Miss Cardenas falling to her knees, confused, disoriented, saying, 'No, no, please—'

Pauline hesitating, then succeeding.

Sofia was already unusually quiet then, wasn't she? The way Emilia had been when she first saw that mannequin move. Things had already been set in motion, but no one else, not even her, was paying close attention.

Alma said, 'I think Sofia's avoiding us because of the university results.'

That wasn't it, but someone had to guess. Since Lucas was attending the private high school across the road, he didn't know the extent of it, but Alma convinced him too. Sofia would now take a different route home from school, refuse invitations to stay back to chat at the cafeteria over

cheap sandwiches and diluted orange juice, not speak with
them during class unless absolutely necessary.

Emilia, preoccupied, didn't notice this at all, but it
made sense to her as well when Alma brought it up. Their
high school was academically competitive, and one of its
selling points to parents was having the highest number
of successful applicants to UP, the state university—even
higher than the expensive private high school across the
road. The school publicized it on the bulletin boards, and
students loved boasting about getting into their first-choice
course or campus in the UP system. For Sofia, school
must have suddenly turned into a special circle of hell.
So Emilia joined them when they decided to corner Sofia
and cajole her into going with them to Alma's house
after class.

Years before Alma's death, before they erected tents and
unfolded tables in the backyard so men could play cards at
her wake, Mrs Bartolome had a dining set arranged outside
in the shade against the back of the house, bordered by pink
santan shrubs in green plastic planters. That was where they
sat now, on this nice day, warm and dry, Emilia teetering
on a wooden stool with her back against the cool cement,
drinking Coke and eating potato chips. Sofia was still quiet,
but at least she was sitting with them, smiling at their jokes.
Just like old times.

They had all agreed beforehand to never mention UP,
college, or any of the university results in front of Sofia, but
this embargo didn't last very long. 'My mother's taking me
shopping tomorrow,' Alma said, wiping cheese powder off
her fingers, about to unknowingly open a can of worms.

'Where?' Emilia asked. 'Malolos?'

'No, for once she actually offered to take me to SM. Early graduation gift. I told her I wouldn't want to bring my ratty shirts to UP.'

Lucas, who was sitting next to Sofia, put a hand over his face as the bomb fell.

Alma, feeling the blast, popped her lips and poured more Coke into their glasses. 'Um,' she said. 'Anyway.'

Still no reaction from Sofia, who was staring at Alma's hands.

Joaquin sighed. 'I don't know why we're making such a big deal out of this. Sophie, look, I don't even know if I can go to UP.'

Lucas removed his hand from his face and frowned at him.

'I'll probably stay here. You got into SCC, too, didn't you?'

Silence.

'What the hell are you talking about?' Lucas said.

Joaquin shrugged. 'Maybe my father can afford to pay tuition, but what about lodging and books and all that other stuff? Besides, he wants me to continue helping him out at the shop.'

'But,' Emilia said, unable to stop herself from jumping into the fray, 'you got into engineering. That was your first choice. My parents need help at the store, too, but they still want me to go to the city to study.'

'It'd be a shame if you didn't go,' Lucas said. 'If you need funds for rent, we can get part-time jobs on campus or—'

Joaquin smirked. 'You'd get a job, Mister Private School?'

Lucas rolled his eyes. 'Well, probably not—'

'Ha!'

'But what I'm saying is, there's always a way, right?'

'If you're so sure you're not going,' Alma said, 'why did you even take the UPCAT?'

'Just to see if I can pass the test, I guess,' Joaquin said, smiling. 'And I did. So there's that.'

Alma's eyes widened in response to this. Joaquin mirrored her reaction a moment later, looking stricken. Sofia still had not said a word.

'Sophie,' Emilia said. 'Are you okay?'

Sofia now looked shell-shocked, as though she had heard a loud sound. It took her a while to zero in on Emilia's face. She blinked once, twice. 'What?'

'Are you okay?' Emilia said. 'Do you want something to drink?'

'What?' Sofia said again. She looked at the glass of Coke with wonder, as though it had just materialized in front of her. 'No.'

'I'll just go to the bathroom,' Alma said. Sofia watched her go. Emilia, Joaquin, and Lucas watched her watching.

'Are you sure you're all right?' Joaquin asked.

Alma's backpack was sitting on the table, the zipper open. When the kitchen door swung shut, Sofia reached over to pull the backpack closer to her. She reached in, looking through Alma's things, her movements casual, unhurried, as if she were bored.

They glanced at each other. *What the hell?* Lucas cleared his throat. 'Do you need anything?'

'I don't think you should be doing that,' Joaquin said.

Sofia pulled out a notebook and flipped through it.

'Cut it out,' Emilia said. 'Seriously.'

Her cold stare stopped Emilia from saying anything more. Then Sofia flipped a page and froze.

'What?' Lucas said, attempting to pull the page towards him so he could see. 'What is it?'

Sofia burst out of her chair and thundered into the house. They followed her inside, found her knocking on the bathroom door, gripping the notebook with her other hand. 'Open up!' she shouted. 'Open up! Open up!'

The bathroom door opened. 'What the hell's going on?' Alma demanded.

'Who are you?' Sofia shouted. She sounded angry. Frightened.

'What?' Alma said.

'Who are you?' She shoved a page of the notebook to her face, pointing, 'Why do you have this with you?'

'What do you mean?'

'This!' Sofia looked down at the page and stopped talking abruptly. They followed her gaze.

Sofia was pointing at a blank page. Alma looked at Emilia, at Lucas, at Joaquin, as though begging them all to explain. 'That's just the notebook where I write notes for bio.'

'But I—' Sofia said, forefinger still on the empty page. 'I—'

Joaquin reached over, closed the notebook, and handed it back to Alma.

Sofia looked ready to burst into tears. 'Oh, God,' she said. Emilia placed a hand gently on her back, between her shoulder blades. Sofia's back felt as stiff as a board. 'I'm so sorry,' Sofia said.

'I can't believe you went through my things,' Alma said. 'What the hell's the matter with you?'

The floor of the butcher shop, unlike the rest of the wet market, was covered with white tiles, the grout dark with old blood. Emilia stepped inside. Each butcher had his own table and circular chopping block, and his own set of customers bickering with him regarding the quality of his cut, adding to the constant din of the market, their voices like rushing water. She spotted Joaquin standing at the back behind his own table, his face partly obscured by the meat hanging from hooks—ribs, legs, entrails.

'Miss?' The butcher to her right was waiting for her to order. 'Which cut?'

'Uh.' She looked over at Joaquin, who was still with a customer. 'I'll wait.'

The butcher followed her gaze. 'Someone's looking for you,' he shouted at Joaquin, smiling now. 'A girl!'

Jeers and laughter from the other butchers.

Joaquin looked up and met Emilia's gaze. He bagged the meat for the customer and stepped away from his table to approach her.

His apron was made from an old flour sack. Emilia could see the logo at the hem, sideways, following the cut of the sack, sun-faded and stitched with another piece of cast-off fabric.

His hands left red streaks on his apron. 'Pig's blood,' he said, when he saw her looking. 'Are you buying anything?'

'We're just outside,' she replied. Joaquin had a cut above his left eyebrow, a bruise on the side of his face the colour of mossy water. She couldn't help but stare. 'What happened to your face?'

What's her name? What's her name? The other butchers, older than Joaquin, elbowed each other. Snickered behind fists. 'Hi, miss.'

She glanced at them, hesitated.

He took off his apron and balled it up, threw it at the butcher who first spoke to her. 'I'm taking a break.'

Woo! Happy exclamations. As though Joaquin had won something. Then: 'Wait, you can't leave yet! Your father will look for you!'

He led her away from the shop towards the river, weaving between the stalls of fresh fish and oysters, between plastic vats filled with the day's catch. They met up with Alma and Lucas and stopped at an eatery. Stews boiled in large steel pots. Fishermen and tricycle drivers wiped their faces with towels already wet with sweat and river water. An elderly woman, her white hair in a bun, greeted Joaquin by name, led them to a table in the corner with little plates carrying calamansi and a small container of soy sauce. She came back with four steaming bowls of beef noodles, the soup thick and dark, and sweating bottles of Coke, the straws folded into the lip of the bottles to protect them from flies.

'She buys meat from our shop,' he explained. 'So I get free snacks.'

He added soy sauce, squeezed the halved calamansi. His movements slow, imprecise.

'Are we just not going to talk about the bruise on your face, then?' Lucas said.

Joaquin shook his head. 'It's nothing. An accident. I got up too quickly this morning.' He looked around the table. 'So? I still think we should tell her father.'

It had been three days since Sofia's outburst.

'I don't know how he's going to react,' Lucas said. 'He's awful. I wouldn't be surprised if we find out he hits her.' He stared at Joaquin's bruise while saying this. Joaquin just kept eating, the steam from the bowls making his cheeks weep.

A group of young men passed by their table. 'Hi, sexy,' one of them said, staring at Emilia and Alma. To Joaquin: 'You should introduce us next time.'

Lucas' chair scraped against the cement floor as he started to get up, but Joaquin grabbed his arm, pulled him down. 'You don't want to do that, boss. It's not worth it.'

Alma crossed her arms, waited until the men were out of earshot, and then said, 'Sophie spoke to me after what happened. She said she saw symbols in my notebook. Symbols. What the hell does that even mean?'

Emilia took a sip of her soup. 'She told us that when we were walking her home.'

'Did she tell you about the house?'

This hit Emilia like a lance. 'What?' She put down her spoon. 'What house?'

'She was rambling on about this story that made no sense. She said there was a girl taking a walk one morning, and she found an empty house in a field. Except the house wasn't empty. Whoever lived in the house wanted a gift. Or something.'

Emilia felt as if she had just been gutted, like the fish twitching in their vats.

'She's clearly having some sort of mental breakdown,' Joaquin said. 'We need to tell someone. If not her father, maybe the guidance counsellor. We need to ask for advice. None of us knows how to deal with something like this.'

'Ever since she screamed at me,' Alma said, 'I can hear a sound playing in my head.'

They all turned to her. 'What do you mean?' Lucas said. 'Like tinnitus?'

Joaquin mimicked the sound: '*Eeeeee*. Something like that? Like a high-pitched sound?'

Alma squirmed in her seat, scratched the side of her neck. 'Like music,' she said. 'Like a piano playing, but the volume's turned down low. At first, I thought it was just my cell phone. An alarm. A radio someone forgot to turn off. But it's relentless.'

'You can hear it here?' Emilia said. 'Right now?'

Alma nodded and hummed a few bars of melody none of them recognized. 'I'm going insane, aren't I?' she said. 'I'm going insane like Sophie.'

Joaquin handed her some table napkins. 'It will be okay, Al,' he said, agitated by her sudden tears. 'Please don't cry.'

Emilia woke up in the middle of the night and realized she was being embraced by Pauline's black goat. She could feel its heavy foreleg around her waist, its hoof resting on her stomach. Its belly warm against her back, wet snout nuzzling her nape. Horns scratching the headboard.

She began to breathe fast, hyperventilating, the edges of her vision starting to turn grey. Kneeling next to the bed, her face just inches away, was Miss Cardenas. She appeared to Emilia as she last remembered her. Short bob, rimless glasses, immaculate eyeliner, lips lined with pink lip gloss.

'You know what happened to us, don't you?' she asked, gesturing with a small nod of her head at the goat lying next to Emilia.

Emilia couldn't speak, couldn't breathe properly.

'I heard behind me a great voice, as of a trumpet,' Miss Cardenas said. 'And I turned to see the voice that spoke with me. What did I see?'

The black goat's foreleg moved up to her chest and settled like a heavy log.

'What is the divine but that which is beyond understanding or explanation?' Miss Cardenas held out her hand and showed her a smooth pebble resting on her palm. 'If I made this pebble disappear, then this act would violate the laws of physics. The first law of thermodynamics states that energy can neither be created nor destroyed, only altered. I can make this pebble disappear by letting it drop back to the ground. That follows the laws of physics. But if I make it disappear into thin air, won't you ask, "Where did it go?" Because you are governed by the laws of the physical world. You know the rules, and you have no choice but to follow them. And so you ask, "Where did it go?" Because it has to go somewhere, doesn't it, Lia? It has to. And if you ask this and I say, "It is nowhere, it is no longer of this world, it has ceased to exist," what will you feel?'

Emilia shook her head. She knew this wasn't Miss Cardenas, and this wasn't Pauline's goat embracing her from behind.

'I'd look for the trick,' Emilia replied.

Miss Cardenas didn't seem to like this answer. Her voice hardened, 'There is no trick.'

'I would—' The goat's foreleg on her chest, stroking her. She couldn't breathe.

Miss Cardenas asked again, pebble in her hand, 'What will you feel?'

'Fear.' Emilia didn't hesitate this time. She looked away from Miss Cardenas' eyes to glance at her hand, and the pebble was gone.

'What else?'

'Awe,' Emilia said.

Miss Cardenas nodded, looking almost teary-eyed with pleasure, or relief. 'That's it. That's it, that's it, that's it, that's it.'

In the years since it happened, Emilia had settled on her own mythology, a stable worldview upon which she could rest her life: The only life that matters is the life you have now. The universe doesn't operate on moral judgments; hence a paedophile may survive a car crash but not the kind grandmother seated next to him, simply because she had cracked her head open, and he did not. Goat iconography has appeared throughout the ages and is not inherently evil. He is Pan. He is Heidrun. He is Baphomet. He is Shub-Niggurath.

And yet—

And yet.

Sofia asked them to meet her at home at 9 p.m., when her father would be asleep.

She and her father had danced this dance for so many years. She knew every habit, every quirk, every move. The alarm going at 5 a.m., a leisurely breakfast with coffee, pandesal, and the morning news, a quick dash to the shower, out the door before 7 a.m., home by 5 p.m., in bed by 9 p.m. And in between, unheard, unseen, Sofia getting ready for the day at her own pace.

'I have something important to tell you,' she said.

'Something you can't say in front of your father?' Lucas said. 'Why not just tell us now?'

Sofia looked around the school grounds from the front gate where they were huddling, watching all the students moving about. She looked panicked. 'No' was the only response she gave before shuffling away. That was all she could tell them now. Take it or leave it.

They still had not spoken to any adult about Sofia, and, despite their constant urging after her confession in the market, Alma still had not gone to her parents or the doctor regarding the strange melody she was hearing in her head.

Emilia could not blame her. She herself still had not told them about Pauline, about the possible connection with what's happening with Sofia, about her dark suspicions. Everything felt overwhelming, everything felt like a secret that had to be kept. Every day she was the young girl stepping into a dark toolshed with her friends, smelling perfume over the smell of shit but not saying a word. Every day was the absolute last day to say something, an ultimatum that kept moving, changing. She would soothe herself, knowing that in a few months they would be moving to the city. Or at least she would. She just needed to hold on until then, and all this madness would be behind her.

At 9 p.m., Emilia gathered with her friends outside Sofia's gate, staring at the same view she would be staring at over Michelle's dashboard twelve years later—dirty kitchen, washing machine, clothesline, tubs for rainwater. To her surprise, Lucas showed up wearing an SCC shirt and basketball shorts, hair tangled with sweat.

'There was a game,' he said when he noticed her staring.

'Tonight?' Emilia said. 'On campus?'

'You play basketball?' Joaquin asked.

'Yes, I play basketball,' Lucas said. 'There's a game on every other night at the high school. Why do you look so surprised?'

'I can't imagine you on a basketball court,' Emilia said. 'You're more of a—what's that sport that rich Americans play, Joaquin?'

'Polo?' Joaquin said, laughing now.

'Lacrosse?'

'How else can I stay out this late if I don't join the game?' Lucas crossed his arms. 'I have to tell my mother something.'

Emilia shrugged. 'We told our parents we're at your house.'

'Oh, Jesus Christ.'

Alma, fingers wrapped around the bars of the gate like a prisoner, shushed them, and they had to stifle their laughter.

When Sofia finally appeared, she looked as if she were sleepwalking, eyelids drooping, a pattern from her embroidered pillowcase still visible on her cheek, as though she had just rolled out of bed. She opened the gate and let them in. They didn't speak as they followed her, as if they were hushed by her presence, as if they were walking into a church. The spell broke when they heard Sofia's father, his snores so loud they could have rattled the windowpanes. Joaquin even chuckled, Lucas saying a whispered, 'Wow'. Alma hit a chair leg on the way in, the chair scraping against the floor—a half-second of panic crossing Sofia's face as the snores paused—but moments later, the old man just resumed his thunder-like snoring.

'What are we doing here, Sophie?' Joaquin said, lowering his voice, even though Sofia's old man sounded as if he could have slept through gunfire.

'Once there was a girl,' she said, 'taking a walk through an empty field, and she found an empty house in a field. But the house wasn't empty. Whoever lived in the house—'

They took her in, her red-rimmed eyes, the tremor in her fingers.

'Is your father hurting you, Sophie?' Joaquin asked.

'We've been talking about this,' Emilia jumped in, speaking quickly before she lost her nerve, 'and you know you can always stay over at my house, right?'

But Sofia wasn't listening to her. She was looking at Joaquin, at the bruise on the side of his face starting to fade to yellow.

'Your father hits you,' she said.

Emilia glanced at Joaquin. It felt as if something had exploded in the living room, but everything remained quiet, Sofia's father still snoring, no one moving a muscle.

'I just hit my face when I got up too quickly,' Joaquin said. But his voice was too small, too hesitant.

'You told him about your big plan of studying in the city, and that's how he answered you. Same way he always does.'

'No,' Joaquin insisted. 'It was an accident.'

Sofia took on the speech cadence of Joaquin's father when she responded, 'And how do you propose to pay for the fees, then? You'll go running to your favourite aunt again, tell her I'm a stubborn bastard who doesn't know anything about the world besides butchering animals? Well, Engineer Joaquin, this stupid butcher put your aunt through school, and now just because she lives in the city and works in an office, she thinks she can lord it over me. But every fiesta she comes here ordering meat and puts them on a tab she never pays. Do you expect her to help you? Engineer Joaquin? That just shows how smart you are.'

Emilia looked over to see how Joaquin was reacting to all this, and flinched when she saw that he was crying. Lucas reached over to touch his shoulder.

'Was that what his father said?' Alma asked. 'How did you know all that?'

Sofia walked through the doorway towards the bedrooms. Alma followed her, but everyone else remained in the living room, Joaquin wiping his face.

'Was everything she said true?' Lucas asked.

'I want to get out of here,' Joaquin said.

They had never seen him cry. Emilia was devastated. Terrified.

'Okay,' Lucas said. 'You got it, boss.'

What else was there to say?

'I don't really understand what's going on here,' Lucas said. 'Maybe we should just go.'

Emilia nodded. 'I'll go grab Alma.' But before she could do anything, Alma had already run back to them, framed by the doorway, slapping an open palm on the wall to get their attention.

'She's got a knife,' Alma said, eyes wide. 'A knife, a knife, a knife.'

They hastened down the corridor, Sofia taking brisk steps ahead of them. They could see her holding a knife with the blade pointing downward. A sharp turn and she was in her father's bedroom. They ran. They saw Sofia standing next to her father's bed holding the knife above her head, then a movement so quick they didn't even have a chance to register it, didn't even have a chance to say *No* or *Wait* or *What are you doing.*

Sofia walked out and sank to the floor outside her father's door, holding the knife now dripping with blood. They sat in front of her in the corridor, their backs against the opposite wall. Emilia could hear Lucas breathing hard, and realized she was doing the same.

Inside the room, Sofia's father was screaming. They could hear the creaks on the floor, the loud thud as the old man fell from the bed. They couldn't see Sofia's father from where they sat, but they could see blood all over the room, staining the pillows, the tangled-up sheets.

The old man was screaming as if he had been set on fire.

Alma was crying. Loud, hiccupping sobs. The rest of them were too shocked to do or say anything.

'This should be enough,' Sofia whispered, and at first Emilia thought she was asking her a question and was waiting for an answer. But Sofia kept repeating herself, words whispered under her breath like a prayer, 'This should be enough. This should be enough. This should be enough. This should be enough.'

Out of nowhere, Pauline's words, sailing through the fog: *Did you know I tried to give it one of my mother's necklaces?*

Emilia's hands shook. She couldn't seem to catch her breath.

Sofia was staring at her, suddenly looking as if she had just awakened. 'Help!' she screamed, dropping the knife on the floor, and running down the corridor, back to the living room. 'Help us!'

'What?' Lucas said. 'What is she doing?'

They heard her burst through the front door.

'We need to get out of here,' Emilia said. Her friends had already sprung to their feet, ready to run. 'We need to get out of here.' But she couldn't move.

Joaquin and Lucas had to help her up, steady her, holding one arm each as they hobbled to the exit. She was shivering too much, as though the temperature in the house had dropped. *Precious doesn't mean expensive.* An invective she couldn't shake.

'Oh, God,' Alma said, hands over her ears. 'Oh my God.'

'It's okay,' Lucas whispered. 'We're okay. Just keep moving.' They left through the back door. They could still hear Sofia screaming outside, begging for help.

Emilia arrived home about an hour later. A lifetime later. She lay her head on her pillows, wide-awake and shivering for hours until her mother knocked on her door at 3 a.m. She announced that Emilia would have to accompany her to open the store because her father was feeling sick.

The errand would have annoyed her on a regular day, but not today. Today, she felt relieved. She knew she wouldn't be able to sleep anyway. She welcomed the distraction, the reminder of her simple and normal life.

News travelled fast through the market. Several horrified customers told her mother about what happened to Sofia's father. Someone had broken into his home and cut up his face, they said, two deep slashes from forehead to cheek, cutting through his eyelids and eyeballs. The man's poor daughter heard him screaming in the middle of the night and called for help. He was now in the local hospital, in critical condition. It sounded so monstrous that at first nobody could react.

Then: *Was it a robbery? Who would do such a thing? Did he have a fight with someone?*

Everyone agreed it was a strange thing to do, cutting a man's face instead of stabbing him. An angry gesture.

'Whoever did it must have been very angry.'

'Or maybe he was just interrupted.'

'But cutting a man's eyes—that's not exactly the first thing you think of doing, do you, if you're holding a knife? He must have really planned to blind him.'

'I heard he had been hallucinating. He kept saying he saw a woman in a white dress and a black veil standing over him when it happened, but how could he even see, if his eyes were cut up like that?'

The wave of customers ebbed at ten in the morning, and Emilia's mother heaved a sigh of relief, sat down, and ate her breakfast of dried fish, eggs, and rice. Emilia said she would just buy a roast beef sandwich from the Burger Machine nearby, but turned to the direction of the river, to the butcher shop.

Lucas, apparently, had the same idea.

'My mother asked me to get some pork,' he said, holding a plastic bag of eggplants and cabbage heads. He had freshened up, changed out of his basketball clothes.

Sure she did. Emilia said nothing.

Joaquin was looking at the floor when they approached the counter. 'What can I get for you today?' Emilia spotted the fresh bruise on the side of his face when he looked up. A deep, angry purple on top of the previous yellow stain. Joaquin saw her staring, cleared his throat, gestured to the meat hanging from the hooks above him. 'Pork or beef?'

For a moment, neither Emilia nor Lucas could say anything. Emilia imagined Joaquin sneaking back into the house late at night, shaken to the core by what they had all witnessed, his father's fist coming fast and unseen.

The cuts of meat and the smell of blood made Emilia gag.

'I don't want to talk about it,' Joaquin said as they continued staring at the bruise. 'Okay?'

Lucas took a deep breath. 'Then let's talk about what happened last night.'

'What do you mean?' Joaquin said.

Lucas looked about ready to explode. 'What do you mean what do I mean?'

'Didn't I tell you that we should have told someone about her?' Joaquin shot back. Angry now, looking as if he wanted more than anything to jump over the counter and choke Lucas on the floor. 'For God's sake,' voice lowered to a whisper, 'you saw what she did.'

'And what about what she said to you?' Lucas said. 'About your father. How could she have known that? Did you tell her?'

'Of course I didn't tell her.'

'Then how?'

'You're back!' One of the other butchers sidled up to Joaquin, smiling at Emilia. 'Hi, miss.'

Emilia felt the prickly sensation of embarrassment and annoyance flow across her face. 'We're talking to our friend here.'

The man ignored her. To Joaquin: 'When are you going to introduce us to this beauty?'

It took Emilia several seconds before she could piece together what happened next—Joaquin's frightened *No*; Lucas pulling the butcher by the collar of his shirt and throwing him to the tiled floor; the butcher, shouting in surprise, falling hard on his elbows; and now Lucas was on him, punching his face over and over, the blood from the butcher's nose and his injured lips mingling with the blood of butchered meat.

Several people had to jump in before they could pull Lucas and the butcher apart from each other, with Emilia, in the ensuing confusion, receiving a blow to the shoulder that she was sure would also bruise.

She would soon be well-acquainted with the antiseptic din of hospitals—the drone and hiss of medical instruments, the startling sound of nurses' laughter in the midst of human catastrophe—but that day was her first time to step into an emergency room. At the entrance before the driveway sat a makeshift sari-sari store, the storekeeper sitting on a plastic chair inside thin walls made of pieces of plywood and cut-up tarpaulin. The storekeeper was selling bags of potato chips, ham and cheese sandwiches cut into triangles and individually wrapped, drinks packed in ice in a cooler.

Emilia was at first affronted by the lack of urgency in their case. She thought nurses would descend from their stations right away to look after Lucas and the young butcher, but it was as if they had just strolled into a random building lobby, with people sitting on uncomfortable modular pod seats, waiting and staring into space. Later, it would make sense to her that no one would be running to assist them; in a hospital serving several townships, bleeding cuts and bruises were low on the totem pole of things-to-deal-with.

The waiting area was dark and quiet, but beyond the rows of chairs, the ER was chaos, packed with so many sick people there was no longer room to hang privacy curtains between the beds. An old man in a wheelchair, dishevelled and hooked up to an IV, gestured to anyone who passed by. His was the deep brown skin of someone who had spent years of his life working under the sun. Emilia wondered what had led him to this wheelchair, to this lonely corner of the ER where they had sequestered patients who couldn't pay for a private room. He was thirsty, he gestured. No one cared.

Emilia sat between Lucas and his adversary, enduring several minutes of humiliation as Joaquin's and Lucas' fathers spoke to each other about the young men in their care and how one of them 'was just defending this young woman's honour', hand gesturing towards her general direction. She was trying her best to tune him and everyone else out, but when someone asked if she would like them to call her parents, she responded with such a forceful 'No!' that it made some people turn their heads in surprise.

Joaquin's father was a tall, bulky boulder of a man compared to Lucas' willowy father, wearing a crisp, white shirt, rimless glasses perched on his nose. Joaquin's father had shed his apron but kept his towel, drenched in sweat and market smells, around his neck. Emilia imagined him throwing all of his muscle and weight behind a punch, Joaquin's face on the receiving end of it, and wished she could hit him in a way that would hurt.

'Now what vile thing did you say to this young lady, you stupid bastard,' Joaquin's father said.

The younger butcher, covering his bleeding face with a clean apron he had grabbed on the way out of the shop, spluttered an explanation to his boss, 'I swear I didn't say anything—I just said hi and he just grabbed me and he kept—'

Lucas' father offered to pay for everyone's hospitals bills as long as they could settle this issue like gentlemen.

'Lia,' Lucas said.

The plastic seat was digging into the back of her knees. Emilia stood up just to stretch her legs but found herself walking out of the emergency room altogether and heading towards a wide door marked TO HOSPITAL LOBBY.

A splutter of surprise from the men, followed by a small commotion as Lucas stood up to follow her. 'Lia, wait.' He was drawing looks from the people waiting in the lobby. He didn't have it as bad as the butcher, but his knuckles were bruised and swollen, and his face was covered with bleeding cuts.

'Happy now?' Emilia said, still walking. 'Did you get it out of your system?'

'I don't know what happened,' he said. 'I'm sorry. He was so smug and disrespectful to you and I just snapped and—'

'Decided to defend my honour?' Emilia scoffed. 'Great job. You better go back there then, I think your father will insist we marry now.'

He looked pained. 'Come on. It's not like that.'

'Looks like you enjoyed it, too, you know? Defending my goddamn honour? Are you sure this whole thing is even about me? Do you think this is what I want to do, spend my whole afternoon in the emergency room?'

'Please, I said I'm sorry.' He looked as if he were about to cry. 'Where are you going?'

The woman at the reception desk, who had been listening to their conversation, tried to hide her amused smile when Emilia approached. 'How can I help you?' she said. She glanced at Lucas and pointed to the right. 'The emergency room is that way, sir.'

'I know, we were just there,' Lucas said.

'You might want to go back there, sir, you're dripping blood on the floor.'

'I'm looking for a patient,' Emilia said, and gave the name of Sofia's father.

He was moved to a private room after the surgery. They walked down to the end of a narrow corridor and into a room with peeling walls and a TV mounted on the wall whispering a car commercial.

Sofia was sitting next to her father's bed, facing the window on the opposite wall. Weak sunlight streamed through the grimy blinds, the tilt wand knotted up with the cords.

Sofia didn't even move when they opened the door; she just stared out the window at nothing. Emilia was surprised to see Joaquin and Alma already there.

'Oh my God,' Alma said, holding a hand to her mouth when she saw Lucas.

'What are you doing here?' Joaquin said. 'Why did you leave the ER?' He stood up and grabbed Lucas by the shoulders, attempting to steer him away. 'You need to get yourself looked at. I think you broke your hand.'

'I didn't break my hand. Calm down, will you?'

'You're telling *me* to calm down?'

Sofia said nothing at all. She sat still in her chair, eyes looking out the window as her father's chest rose up and down, up and down, the machines surrounding his bed and attached to his arms beeping and blinking, his face wrapped with bandages.

A flash of memory—the glint of Sofia's knife, a sudden movement—made Emilia sick to her stomach.

'What do you have to say for yourself?' Emilia said. The room fell silent, Joaquin and Lucas abruptly ending their bickering by the door.

Sofia turned her head towards the voice.

'You hated your father,' Emilia said. 'You wanted to blind him. And then—and then what? You decided you wanted an audience? And at the eleventh hour realized that you had gone completely insane? Did you want company in jail too? So you just pulled us all into it, maybe try to get us all arrested?'

'Keep your voice down, Lia,' Alma said. A moment later, glancing at Joaquin, she continued, 'We've been trying to talk to her about it, but she won't say anyth—'

'You know why I did it,' Sofia said.

On the TV, the commercials had given way to an afternoon lifestyle feature about a politician's horse stables in Santa Ana Park. The host's saccharine voice cut through the silence in the room. Joaquin reached up to switch the TV off.

'Don't give me that bullshit about a goddamn house,' Emilia said.

Sofia looked as surprised as she felt after she said it.

'Don't you dare,' Emilia continued. 'Don't start on that like Pauline did. You hated your father, and you wanted to hurt him. There was no other reason, no other motivation.' She gestured at the bed. 'Now stop making excuses. Own this, because you did it. You blinded your own father. Congratulations. You monster.'

Sofia looked away, as though slapped by that word. *Monster.* She fidgeted with the hospital bedsheet, rolling the white fabric between her fingers. She mumbled something Emilia couldn't hear.

'What?'

'You saw it move,' Sofia said.

Terror spiked up her back. 'No, Sophie.' The concave shape of a black veil over a rubber mouth that shouldn't be expelling air. 'Shut up.'

'You saw it with your own eyes. Pauline showed you. You saw it breathe. You can't explain that away. You know.' Hand on her chest. 'I know.'

'Wait,' Joaquin said. 'I'm confused. What did Pauline have to do with any of this?'

'You saw *what* move?' Lucas said. 'What is Sophie even talking about?'

Sofia looked triumphant. 'You haven't told them,' she said. 'Why? Because you're afraid. Like me.' Tears fell down her face. 'Because you know it's true.'

Now Emilia had to tell them. Now she had to sit down in the hospital cafeteria after Lucas had the cuts on his face looked at and his right hand put in a splint ('Sprained, not broken,' Lucas said with a roll of his eyes when Joaquin clocked it, shaking his head). Now she had to replay the scenes she had shoved to the back of her mind: Pauline with her goat screaming in fear in front of that house, the mannequin wearing Mia's white chiffon dress, *First, you need to give it something that is precious to you, then it needed a shelter, a doorway*, the mannequin breathing, Emilia running away in terror. And a realization that dawned upon her in the process of narration, an insight that she had never entertained before: the last step, the—*say it, Emilia*—sacrifice—it was meant to be her. That was why Pauline had asked her to come that night, why she grabbed her wrist so tightly, why she was crying when she turned to her and said, 'You believe me now.' But Emilia ran, and perhaps during the chase afterwards, Pauline lost her nerve, or realized, even behind that veil of madness, that she still cared for her friend after all, and turned to poor Miss Cardenas instead.

'She said, be ready for a life of good fortune. She said, it can't bring my sister back. So she did all of that because she was asking for something.'

'And in return, you had to kill someone?' Joaquin said.

'Wait,' Lucas said, his splint click-clacking on the tabletop as he put his hands before him, reaching towards Emilia. 'You're saying that Pauline killed Miss Cardenas?'

'A week after that, we heard that Miss Cardenas was missing and Pauline's father was recovering from surgery.'

An incredulous, humourless *Ha!* from Lucas. 'You can't be serious.'

'It can't bring her sister back, but it cured her father,' Emilia said. 'I know how crazy this sounds, okay? Why do you think it took me this long to tell you? True or not, Pauline believed it. Now, Sofia believes it. She believes it so much she,' her voice lowered to a whisper, 'blinded her own father.'

'But you did see it move,' Alma said. 'You said you saw the mannequin breathe.'

'Maybe Pauline drugged her,' Joaquin said. He turned to Emilia, 'Did she give you anything to eat or drink before you saw all of that?'

'Okay, let's say this is all true,' Lucas said. 'What was Sofia asking for?' He looked around the table. 'A spot in UP so we can all go to the same university? Come on.'

'To get away from her father,' Joaquin said.

Lucas started to scratch the back of his head and winced, remembering his injury. 'She already cut up his face,' he said. 'She could have just as easily murdered him. She didn't need any help, if that's all she wanted.'

'Maybe she's not asking for anything,' Alma said, cupping her ears. 'Maybe she's just doing it because she doesn't want it to hurt her. Maybe she doesn't have a choice after all.'

'This is insane,' Lucas said.

'More insane than four hundred people dancing themselves to death?' Alma said.

They fell silent. Suddenly they were back in the Science Garden, daring each other to enter the haunted toolshed.

'Where is this house?' Lucas said.

'No,' Emilia said, making them jump in surprise.

But Joaquin was looking at Lucas, thinking. 'She wants us to see it,' Joaquin said. 'Maybe this is the only way to convince her—'

'No, you are not going there. No. No. You are not going anywhere near that house.'

She knew she was screaming. She knew everyone in the small cafeteria—the sleep-deprived nurses, the patients waiting for awful news, the family members waiting for a surgery to end, her friends holding up their hands to calm her down—were staring at her in alarm, but she couldn't stop screaming.

'You are not going there. Do you hear me? Promise me. We need to stop talking to her. She's doing something evil, and we can't stop it and you are not going anywhere near that house. Promise me you will never go anywhere near that house.'

She couldn't breathe. Everything was turning grey. Suddenly she was sitting on the floor, the chair overturned next to her, and someone wearing scrubs was instructing her to calm down, 'Miss, breathe with me, in and out, that's right, that's it, in and out, in and out.'

What was it that would eventually make them go to that house?

First a splinter, then a wall caving in.

Joaquin was late returning to the butcher shop after the scene at the hospital, and his father threw a chair aimed at his head. He missed. His father did this in full view of his workers, in full view of the people milling around the market. What if he didn't miss?

If he could inflict a life-destroying injury with an audience, what else could he do in private?

Joaquin sneaking a phone call like a victim on the run. 'Lucas, listen—'

'I know,' Lucas said, his voice tiny, reticent. 'My father won't shut up about it. I know I messed up. I don't need a talking-to right now, okay?'

'Can I come over?'

A small beat. 'What happened?' Even though Lucas already knew what had happened. Or he could guess. Of course, Joaquin could come over.

He had now spent three nights in a row at Lucas', in the guise of schoolwork or helping around the house, as Joaquin's father was becoming more and more violent.

Joaquin's father respected the Chans, or rather, respected their money, their status in town, and said nothing whenever Joaquin told him he was spending the night at their house. *Make yourself useful*, he would say.

Lucas' parents, on the other hand, seemed overly deferential towards Joaquin's father and his assumed wisdom of the common man's hardships.

Lucas was embarrassed by all this. Joaquin, for his part, didn't quite know how to feel, didn't quite have the words to describe it. He felt self-conscious in their house surrounded by their beautiful things, a bit irritated that he was being treated like a charity case, and ashamed that he would respond like this to another family's kind-heartedness. The emotions just got jumbled up.

'How are you boys doing?' Mr Chan asked. They were having dinner. Roast chicken, rice, green beans, and some leftover pork dumplings arranged on the table, Lucas and

Joaquin still in their school uniforms, Lucas' mother pouring them apple juice. It was raining, the sound of the light drizzle floating in, but instead of feeling cozy, Joaquin felt antsy. It was now a week after the nightmare in Sofia's house, after the incident in the butcher shop, after Emilia hyperventilated in the hospital cafeteria, after his father threw a chair aimed at his head. Lucas still had bruises on his face. How would you answer a question like this?

'Good,' Lucas said.

Joaquin just smiled and nodded.

'And how is your father, Joaquin?'

'He's well, thank you for asking,' Joaquin said.

'I met him, you know,' Mr Chan said, beaming at his wife, like a fan recounting an encounter with a celebrity. 'Salt of the earth, an admirable man.'

Once, his father slapped Joaquin so hard, his left ear started to ring. *Eeeeeee.* Maybe not unlike the melody playing in Alma's head.

Joaquin pushed green beans around on his plate as Lucas rolled his eyes.

'We're so grateful to him for not making a bigger deal out of what happened, Lucas clobbering his employee like that.'

'Pa,' Lucas said.

'I know you're just doing it to protect your friend, but still, a shameful display—'

'It's not shameful if it's justified,' Joaquin said.

The table fell silent.

'He's a jerk and he's disgusting to the women who come to the shop,' Joaquin said. 'He's bound to be punched in the face sooner or later. I'm surprised Lia didn't make a bigger deal out of it. She should have punched him too.'

It was the greatest number of words Joaquin had said in the presence of Lucas' parents. Lucas saw the look of shock on his father's face and snort-laughed into his fist.

'I'm sorry.' Joaquin felt like melting to the floor.

'Oh, don't apologize,' Mr Chan said. 'But, son, you know we don't condone violence in this house.'

'Right,' Joaquin said. 'Of course, sir.'

'How is Lia?' Mrs Chan asked. Joaquin liked Mrs Chan. She was always beautiful and fragrant and gentle. She also hardly spoke during dinner, so when she asked the question, it was as if a delicate porcelain statue had come to life. Joaquin nearly jumped out of his skin.

'She's—' they hadn't spoken to her since the hospital, so Joaquin had to pause to think of what to say, '—fine.'

'Isn't it just awful what happened to your friend's father?' she continued. 'Sofia?'

'Your mother's worried someone's prowling around town, waiting to break in to cut up people's eyes.'

'It is heinous.'

Lucas and Joaquin looked at each other, looked away.

'The police are still investigating it,' Mr Chan said. 'Right, Ma?'

'Do they have any ideas about who did it?' Lucas asked.

'Oh.' Her expression softened. She reached out to touch Lucas' hair. Joaquin was surprised to see his friend bear this tender gesture without inching away, as he normally would. 'You boys must have been so shaken.'

'I'm sure it's a complete stranger,' Mr Chan said. 'Just someone passing through.'

'A drug addict,' Mrs Chan said. 'Someone insane.'

'This is a quiet town, with gentle people. No one here would think to do something like that.' He smiled. 'There's no reason to worry.'

Joaquin was just thinking of the bodies of students floating down the river but decided not to say anything.

One of the maids walked into the dining room. 'A phone call,' she said, 'from Manila.'

Mr Chan shook his head. 'Your brother again,' he said. A sharp rebuke delivered in Hokkien from his wife, and suddenly they were speaking to each other in the language Joaquin didn't speak and Lucas never learned.

'Please excuse my parents,' Lucas said to Joaquin. 'This always happens.'

A megawatt smile from Mrs Chan, the Hokkien parley coming to an abrupt end. 'Excuse me, boys. I need to take this call.'

Mr Chan looked tormented, watching her leave. She didn't return to finish her dinner.

Lucas had to physically restrain Joaquin from clearing the table.

'Leave it, boss,' he said, as two maids swooped in to grab the plates.

They sat down on the floor in a corner of the cream L-shaped sofa in the living room, Joaquin writing ideas on a notepad for English. They were tackling Edgar Allan Poe's stories, 'The Cask of Amontillado', 'The Black Cat', 'The Tell-Tale Heart', 'The Fall of the House of Usher'. Their teacher didn't want a simple oral report. She wanted them to be creative. For example, they could perform a dating show featuring the characters from Poe's stories. Joaquin and Lucas settled with Twenty Questions. *Are you nervous, very, very dreadfully nervous? Have you borne the thousand injuries of Fortunato as best as you could?*

'Damn it,' Lucas said. 'I like the dating show idea better.'

'You know this schoolwork thing is just a cover, right?' Joaquin said. 'You don't actually need to tutor me?'

'We might as well pretend since you're already here.'

'How does the game go again, Twenty Questions? Just yes or no questions, right?'

Lucas nodded, throwing his hand rubber ball in the air. 'Closed questions only, you can ask up to twenty questions until you figure out the answer.' He gestured with his free hand towards his notepad. 'Doesn't this sound like an assignment your Miss Cardenas would have assigned? I bet the school just recycled the lesson plan she made.'

Joaquin couldn't believe that after everything they had learned and seen, after everything that they had gone through, they were still taking this stupid homework from this stupid class of his stupid school seriously.

One of the maids looked young enough to go to Joaquin's high school. She placed a tray of melons, pineapples, and bananas on the coffee table and scurried away across the sprawling living room before he could say thank you.

What was it that would eventually make them go to that house?

Joaquin followed the ball's arc for a moment. 'Weren't you supposed to be gripping that for your wrist?' When Lucas didn't answer, he said, 'I'm sorry I'm staying here again tonight.'

Was it shame?

'Oh, will you stop,' Lucas said, still throwing the ball up in the air. He kept at it until he fumbled and the ball nearly hit the melons. 'You should just move out permanently.'

Joaquin grabbed the ball from him. 'Where would I go?'

'What do you mean?' Lucas frowned. 'You can stay here.'

'I can't stay here forever.'

'Your aunt, then. Don't you have an aunt in the city?'

Joaquin was starting to feel physically ill, even by just talking about it. 'I can't.'

Well, Engineer Joaquin, this stupid butcher put your aunt through school—

'Why not? What could he do?'

His father could do a lot of things. Drive over, drag him back. Break his jaw. Throw his body into the raging river.

'I can't stay somewhere he knows,' Joaquin said.

Mr Chan popped his head in, his yet-unlit after-dinner cigarette sticking out of the corner of his mouth. 'Boys, you know you can use my office if you need to study.'

'Sure, Pa,' Lucas said, and didn't this also cut Joaquin deep, this easy way other people talked to their own fathers?

Was it longing?

Joaquin didn't want to get away from his father. He wanted the father he remembered when he was little, before his mother died, the one who would kneel in front of him to wipe the dirt off his hands and knees after playing in the backyard. He was still in there, residing in that violent monster—that was the heartbreaking thing, wasn't it?— popping up sometimes when he was just starting to get tipsy, talking about how he missed Joaquin's mother, how he loved her, how proud he was to see Joaquin grow up. Then what? Then Joaquin would, let's say, accidentally hit the corner of the table, making his father's bottles of cheap brandy clink against each other, some minuscule, forgivable moment, and the monster would awaken, his father flying into a blind rage and wrapping his hands around his neck, *you insolent piece of shit.*

'Are you okay?' Lucas asked.

Joaquin sighed. 'I'm fine.' How could he escape if the house he wanted to escape was inside his head? He thought of Sofia. Maybe she felt this way, too, love and hate towards her own father, all jumbled up, swinging from remorseless violence to being torn apart for hurting him. No one else among their friends could understand what they knew in their bones. Maybe that was why she suddenly dropped the knife and screamed for help.

'I think you need to write a script for this Twenty Questions skit,' Lucas said.

Joaquin groaned, crushing the exercise ball against his forehead, making Lucas laugh.

'Should we just play GT Legends?' Joaquin said, gathering up their notes. He glanced at Lucas' wrist brace. 'I mean, should I just play GT Legends and you can watch like a loser?'

Lucas rolled his eyes. 'Fine.'

They moved to Lucas' room, where just a few months ago Lucas and Emilia had packed books and he had handed her something that she at first thought was a dead body stuffed in an empty sack of rice.

Lucas felt a chill that he tried to shake off as he watched Joaquin play the game on the PC. He watched over Joaquin's shoulder, perched on the edge of his bed. After a moment, he grabbed another chair so he could sit closer to him. Onscreen, a red 1968 Chevrolet Corvette careened down the racetrack.

'That mannequin came from me,' he said softly, as though the life-size model Pauline had dressed in her sister's dead clothes was still underneath his bed, awake and listening.

Joaquin, now distracted, asked, 'What?'

'You know, the mannequin,' Lucas continued. 'The one that Emilia said Pauline took to that house.'

Joaquin's red Corvette turned a sharp corner and bounced off a Jaguar turning at the same time. He paused the game.

Lucas stammered a protest, 'You didn't need to stop the—'

'What about the mannequin?' Joaquin asked.

Lucas took a deep breath. 'It was my father's mannequin. The kind you use for anatomy classes. He was going to throw it away or donate it to another teacher, but Pauline saw it and she asked for it.'

'And she dressed it up like a,' Joaquin said, 'like a *rebulto*? Like a Santo Niño statue?'

'I shouldn't have given it to her. It was so weird when she told me she wanted it.'

'Why did you think she wanted it, then? Did you think she was going to keep it in her bed?' Joaquin squinted at him. 'And you still gave it to her?'

'Stop it,' Lucas said. 'Stop laughing. It's not funny.'

'I know,' Joaquin said, sobering up. 'I'm sorry.'

Was it fear?

Was it the imagination of disaster?

'I think my parents are having problems,' Lucas said.

There was something awful happening at their wholesale business, an uncle in Manila embezzling funds, tucking away tens of thousands of pesos here and there, not paying their employees on time. Lucas' mother couldn't sleep, couldn't eat. She had been rapidly losing weight, her clothes becoming baggier. She experienced back spasms that kept her to her bed. Stress, she said, over her brother who was robbing her blind, *can you believe it, my own flesh and blood.*

'I'm sorry to hear that,' Joaquin said.

'I feel embarrassed talking about it. With your father and all—'

'It's not a contest.'

Joaquin un-paused the game, and the red Corvette sped away to complete a lap. 'Have your parents talked to you about it?' he asked.

Lucas scoffed. 'What do you think?'

'You should have learned Hokkien.'

'Jesus, are you my grandmother now?'

They shared a laugh and spent the next few minutes in silence, watching a red car go round and round, the sound of revving engines filling the room.

'Lucas.'

'What?'

'You're not thinking your family's having problems because you gave Pauline the mannequin,' Joaquin said, 'are you?'

The question made Lucas uncomfortable. Joaquin glanced at him, paused the game.

'Why do you keep stopping it?'

'Emilia's story was insane,' Joaquin said. 'Pauline? Murdering Miss Cardenas?'

'Don't you trust Emilia?'

'I can't believe it. What the hell is going on with you? You were the loudest sceptic when she first told us.'

Lucas was undeterred. 'Do you trust her?'

'Of course, I do.'

'Well, don't you believe her?'

'I believe she believes what she saw was real,' Joaquin said. 'Like I said, maybe she was drugged.'

'And Sophie too?' Lucas said. 'What kind of drug would cause a specific hallucination like that?'

'Oh my God.'

'I'm playing Devil's advocate,' Lucas insisted.

Joaquin leaned back and crossed his arms. 'No, you're not. You already believe your position.'

'What if it's true?'

'Maybe the girls are having a shared delusion,' Joaquin said. 'Or they're sick? Actually, legitimately sick. Like maybe they have a brain tumour.'

'All four of them have a brain tumour.'

'I don't know. Maybe. Maybe in Alma's case it's just tinnitus, or a seizure. But isn't that scary enough? Doesn't that sound less insane?'

Lucas stood up and started pacing. 'Do you know my parents spilled pig's blood in the foundation of this house before our house was built?'

Joaquin looked surprised by the sudden topic change. 'Sure, everybody in town does that. It's to protect you from bad spirits. My parents had a chicken killed, but that's only because pigs are expensive—'

'So it's not a feng shui thing,' Lucas said, 'and it's certainly not Catholic. It's pre-Catholic. Pre-colonial.'

'Okay?'

'Do you know that a central Aztec belief is that the universe is created and sustained by the bodies of gods?' Lucas said. 'Their blood, their heads, their fingers, their genitals.

And if the gods themselves can freely part of their flesh and blood to ensure the continuation of the universe, how can humans refuse to part of their flesh and blood for the gods?'

Joaquin was a silent for a moment. 'Lucas, we're not Aztecs.'

Lucas would have laughed if he wasn't so unsettled. 'That's not the point,' he said. 'I'm just saying, it's not as crazy as it sounds. Pauline said whoever lived in that house was very old.'

'Emilia said that Pauline said—'

'What if we're cursed?'

'All right.' Joaquin stood up and grabbed his backpack from the floor. 'I'm going to take a shower and I'm going to go to sleep. Good night.'

'My uncle would never hurt my mother,' Lucas said, blurting out the first thing that came to mind. 'He's her older brother, he supported her her whole life. She was his favourite. Why would he suddenly hurt her like this?'

'People hurt people, Lucas,' Joaquin said. 'Uncles steal and fathers choke you until you lose consciousness. Some men don't need evil spirits to make them do stuff. It's not that hard to believe.'

Was it hopelessness?

Lucas tried not to show the horror on his face, but he appeared to be failing. Joaquin wouldn't meet his gaze.

'Your father did what?'

'Nothing.' Joaquin responding too quickly, shutting him down. 'It was just an example. Don't worry about it.'

'I'm sorry,' Lucas said.

Joaquin sighed. 'Good night, boss. Don't drive yourself crazy.'

Something visited Lucas that night. It was dressed like his mother, who looked like she was dying. Cheeks sunken but hair pinned back with a silver comb, clusters of diamonds and pearls sparkling from earlobes, vain and lovely as always.

He knew it was not his mother, but it looked and sounded exactly like her. So how could he turn her away?

It sat on the edge of his bed, brushed his hair back. 'Ma?' he said, even though he knew this was a lie, accepting the logic of dreams.

'Once,' it said, 'there was a girl who threw flowers into the river, thinking the flowers would suffice as a sacrifice.'

'They're not enough,' Lucas said.

'No, no,' it murmured. 'See? You understand.' It smiled. 'Once, there was a girl who wanted to find a quiet place to grieve her life. She stumbled upon an empty house in a field. Except the house wasn't empty.'

'You're in it.' Lucas wanted to swat its hand away, but he couldn't move.

'Once, there was a boy,' it said, leaning closer, eyes sparkling like the gems hanging from its earlobes, 'who thought he knew everything. Just because he read books every now and then. But he doesn't know that the things he doesn't know could fill a bottomless well.'

He started to cry, tears hot on his cold cheeks.

'Lucas,' it said, caressing his face.

He jumped out of bed, out of his room, and rushed into the guest room across the hallway, where Joaquin was sleeping.

Joaquin's head popped out of the sheets. 'Who's that?'

Lucas sat on the floor with his back against the closed door, breathing hard into his cupped hands.

'What's wrong?' Joaquin asked. 'Are you okay?'

'There's something in my room,' Lucas said.

But of course there was nothing in his room. Joaquin led him back there, thinking it was night terrors, that he was just sleepwalking. Lucas crawled under the sheets and went back to sleep right away.

In grade school, for home economics, the whole class had to learn how to cross-stitch. For his final project, Joaquin chose to cross-stitch Bugs Bunny. The pattern looked easy enough to follow, just three colours, including black to frame the edges. His father hated this project, said the school was useless, teaching boys a skill they didn't need to learn to be successful in life.

Somehow, he ended up cross-stitching a pattern of a house, starting from the edge, and moving up. But he had made a horrible mistake, he did not count the squares, he had started at the wrong point. His mother grabbed the fabric and pulled out the X-shaped stitches with a violence that made him cry. The threads left black stains on the linen. His mother folded the fabric in half, then in half again to find the centre. 'You should have started here,' his mother said. 'Here!' Joaquin hated his mother at that moment, hated how she made him feel as if his every mistake was huge and insurmountable, *Jesus Christ it's just a school project*, but slowly he realized this was not how it happened, he was not awake and this was not real, it couldn't be, his mother was already dead, and wouldn't he give anything to feel her near him once again, comforting even in her brusqueness? *Do not let your father see you cry.* Joaquin looked down at her lap and she was already stitching the house back to life. *Start here*, she had said. His mother lived a hard life and had no time for gentleness, *but you were just helping me, weren't you, Mother? You were just trying to help me.*

Emilia would learn all of this from Joaquin and Lucas, confessions whispered to her while they accompanied her in the hospital waiting room, with both of her parents in dire condition in the ICU.

But that was later.

For now, here were Emilia and Joaquin, sitting on the front steps of the school after class, in the shade away from the afternoon sun, Joaquin speaking to her for the first time since they last saw Sofia, bearing peace offerings of potato chips and some stories from Lucas' household.

Alma and Sofia were not in class. They weren't sure if Sofia had already dropped out of school.

'Will you be staying at Lucas' again tonight?' Emilia asked, opening the bag of potato chips.

'Probably.'

'And your father's fine with it.'

Joaquin was quiet for a while, thinking it over. Finally, he said, 'I'm not sure. I feel like he's going to start asking questions sooner or later.'

'Or insinuate that you boys are doing something,' she hummed, searching for the right word, 'funny.'

Joaquin shot her a look. 'Do people think that?'

Emilia shrugged.

'It actually wouldn't be funny if my father thought that,' Joaquin said, shivering in the humidity.

'I know,' Emilia said, patting his shoulder. 'You should just move out permanently.'

'That's exactly what Lucas said.'

'You should just live with them. His family seems to like you.'

'They have their own problems.' Joaquin had told her about the thieving uncle.

'No one's throwing chairs in that house at least.'

What was it that would eventually make them go to that house?

Was it tenderness?

Emilia would think back to this conversation often. She would wonder why Joaquin didn't tell her that Lucas was starting to think that they were cursed.

But then:

'Enough about me,' he said, shaking the bag of potato chips at her to encourage her to grab more. 'How are you, anyway?'

Her father was sick again this week. Something about his bowels. They needed to go to a hospital in the city to run more tests, to find out more, but her father didn't seem to want to find out more.

'I'm fine,' Emilia said, keeping this news to herself. Perhaps she was joining her father in his magical thinking: *If no one talks about it, it will go away.*

There were small children, grade 1 or grade 2 students, racing around the flagpole. They could hear them yelling and laughing in the distance, the sky still a bright blue despite the late hour.

'I'm planning to ask Lucas' father for a loan,' Joaquin said. 'So I can study in the city.'

'Really?' It was the first good news she had heard in a long while.

Joaquin smiled back. 'Really.'

'I'm so happy for you,' she said. She whooped like the kids around the flagpole, making Joaquin laugh. 'I can't wait to get out of this town.'

They would all be in the house three days later.

How did Sofia lure them there?

While Joaquin and Emilia were dreaming up an exit plan, Lucas was summoned out of class by a nervous-looking aide and directed to the teacher's lounge. 'What's going on?' he asked as they stepped out of the classroom.

His father was standing in the corner of the teacher's lounge, facing a window to the parking lot, mute and unresponsive, surrounded by his fellow teachers sitting on mismatched chairs. A bespectacled older woman touched Lucas' arm and whispered, 'We've been trying to talk to him, but he's just not responding.'

Lucas, suddenly the responsible adult in a room full of overeducated educators, stepped up to his father. 'Pa?' he said, urging him out of his stupor. Upon hearing his voice, his father's face broke into a small smile.

'Anak,' he said.

Lucas placed an arm around his shoulders. 'Are you okay?'

That frozen smile. The other teachers waited in silence. Someone stirred old coffee, the teaspoon clinking against porcelain.

'Should we maybe go home?'

Lucas guided his father out of the school and down the parking lot, fishing the keys out of his father's satchel. He had a student permit, but he had never driven home before, and certainly not while wearing a wrist brace. He peeled off the brace and gritted his teeth against the pain.

He drove his father's black sedan very carefully down the road and stopped by the school gate where Joaquin was already waiting.

'Good afternoon, sir,' Joaquin said out of reflex, smiling until Lucas lowered his window.

'Lucas? What's going on?'

'Get in,' Lucas said.

Joaquin settled in the back seat. 'No wonder this car's moving so slowly,' he said. 'Why are you driving? Is your father okay?'

'I actually don't know,' he replied. 'Pa? Pa, what's going on?'

No response from his father.

'What exactly happened?' Joaquin asked.

'He was just in the teacher's lounge, just standing there. He won't even respond to people.' Lucas glanced at the rear-view mirror. 'What do you think this is? Is he having a stroke? Should I be worried?'

'Maybe we should take him to the hospital.' Silence. 'Lucas, I think your father's crying.'

Lucas glanced at his father and to his shock saw that Joaquin was right.

'Pa, what's going on?' he said. 'You're scaring me here.'

'Your mother's dying, son,' he said, so quickly and so quietly that Lucas at first thought he had heard him wrong.

His mother was sleeping when they got home. Lucas guided his father so he could slip into the sheets next to her, tucking him in bed like a child.

Lucas' father had driven her to the city first thing that morning to see a specialist. His mother's CT scans were still in the lounge, right on top of the coffee table, where just yesterday he and Joaquin were figuring out Twenty Questions for Edgar Allan Fucking Poe. What did any of it matter now?

They brought the scans to Lucas' room, placing them side by side on his desk, and looked through them together. Tumours lighting up like fireworks, balls of malignant light in her lungs, in her bones, in her brain. Lucas felt as if he were watching this scene from outside himself. From far away, the scans looked like maps. Nothing harrowing, just maps. Patterns of bright circles.

In the car, his father had said, 'It's everywhere now. It is too late to stop it. It is too late to do anything.'

'But there has to be something,' Joaquin said now. Lucas walked downstairs, towards the kitchen, Joaquin trailing behind him. 'There's always something. Some new drug. A clinical trial.'

Lucas didn't say anything for a long while, suddenly mute, like his father earlier in the teacher's lounge. He stood in his mother's pristine kitchen, surveying the pantry, trying to think of what *merienda* to concoct. What meal would cheer up his broken parents? 'What am I going to do now?' he found himself saying, and immediately chastised himself. What a selfish thing to say. His poor mother, the pain she must have felt day in and day out, attributing it all to stress and resentment, when in truth her own cells were eating her alive.

But that was the first worry that came to mind, didn't it, Lucas?

What is he going to do now?

Joaquin was relieved when Emilia called back right away.

'Am I glad to hear from you,' he said.

A sigh. 'You texted HELP, in capital letters.'

'Right.'

'But you don't sound like you're dying.'

He and Lucas were in Lucas' room now, Lucas sitting on the windowsill next to a plate of untouched orange slices, his forehead pressed against the glass.

'It's Lucas,' Joaquin said. 'I feel like I'm out of my depth here.'

'What happened?'

Joaquin glanced at his friend, cocooned in his despair, and decided he couldn't hear him anyway so might as well tell another friend what was going on. 'It's his mother.'

In the middle of recounting the events of the afternoon in a rushed whisper, Lucas suddenly said, 'Is that Lia?'

Joaquin nearly dropped his phone in surprise. 'Sorry, boss, I should have asked you first before I—'

Lucas didn't seem upset at all, but he looked confused. 'I didn't know you're talking to her again.'

'Yes.' He lowered his phone. 'I spoke to her today. I just asked her to come over. You'd want to see her, too, right?'

But Lucas was back to being catatonic, staring out the window again.

'Joaquin,' Emilia's voice squeaked from the phone. 'What did he say?'

'Um—'

'Sofia,' Lucas said.

'What?' Joaquin said, surprised. 'You want *Sofia* to come over?'

'No, she's here,' Lucas said, pointing out the window. 'Out there. With Alma.'

Joaquin joined him by the windowsill and saw the two girls standing outside, looking up at them. They had already changed out of their school uniforms, wearing jeans and shirts, their hair combed and tied back, just girls out visiting their friends. Sofia lifted a hand to wave. They waved back. She pointed to her right, mouthed, *Open the door*, grabbed Alma's limp arm, and walked out of view.

'Did you call Sofia?' Joaquin asked, and realized right after he said it what a stupid question it was, Lucas couldn't even lift a finger to eat an orange slice.

'Sofia's there?' Emilia asked.

Joaquin had forgotten she was still on the line. 'Lia, I need to hang up now.'

'Don't talk to her,' she said. 'I'm coming over.'

Sofia and Alma's surprise appearance seemed to have animated his friend. 'How's Lia?' Lucas asked as they sped down the stairs to the front door.

'She's on her way,' Joaquin responded. 'She said we shouldn't talk to Sophie.'

They stopped at the landing. 'What?' Lucas said. 'How do you propose we do that? She's already here.'

Joaquin had thought about it. 'You can go back upstairs, and I'll meet her on my own. Tell her you're sick. Come back another time.'

Lucas' face seemed to have fallen into itself, like a building imploding. 'I'm not the one who's sick.'

Joaquin cursed under his breath as Lucas started to cry.

Sofia must have gotten impatient. The sound of the doorbell reverberated down the hall.

A cheerful voice answered, 'I'm coming!'

Lucas took a deep breath and quickly wiped his face. 'Ma?'

It was a warm evening, but Mrs Chan was wearing a cardigan, white with splashes of shimmering silver, as she shuffled to open the front door.

'What are you doing?' Lucas said in a horrified voice. 'You should be in bed.'

She glanced over her shoulder and frowned. 'I already had a nap that went on for too long,' she said. 'Your father is still in bed, however. You should wake him up or he'll sleep through dinner.'

Joaquin watched his friend's shoulders slump. 'Ma, you should be resting.'

'Oh, don't be so dramatic.' She swiped at his arm, and cooed as she opened the door. 'Who do we have here?'

Joaquin was mesmerized by all this. Mrs Chan seemed like her old self, not at all like someone who was dying soon. If it was already unsettling him, what could Lucas possibly be feeling right now?

Mrs Chan opened the door. The girls were smiling ear to ear, but the smiles looked unnatural to Joaquin. This disturbed him more than anything.

'Good evening, po,' they said in giggly unison. Lucas and Joaquin looked at each other.

'Girls,' Mrs Chan said. 'Come in, come in. Oh, is this a double date?'

Alma glanced at Lucas, stared at the uniform he was still wearing. 'Okay, private school boy.'

'Lucas,' Mrs Chan chided, lightly whacking his chest and tugging at his sleeve. 'You didn't even change into a nice shirt for your visitors.'

'It's okay, Tita,' Alma said, laughing. 'I'm just teasing.'

Joaquin felt like driving his head into a wall. Had he fallen into an alternative universe? What in the world was going on?

Mrs Chan turned to Sofia. 'My dear. How is your father?'

Finally, some familiar ground. Joaquin watched in silence as Sofia went through her usual script that he had heard her use in the hospital. *What happened to him was horrific—Never in a million years—Who could do something like that—He never upset anyone as far as I know—But he's stable—He might need to stay in the hospital for a few more days—I'll be there to support him—I know it will be difficult but he's my father—Thank you for being so kind.*

Her usual bullshit. Which was his brand of bullshit, too, whenever people asked about his own father, right?

They should listen to Lia. They shouldn't be talking to Sofia. He had to get her away from here.

'I'm so glad to hear that,' Mrs Chan was saying now. 'You are a strong and beautiful young woman.' She touched her cheek. 'I feel for your father. No parent would want their child to witness their suffering like this.'

The silence that followed stretched to an uncomfortable length. Sofia did not fill it with more of her pleasantries.

'Ma,' Lucas said.

'Oh, of course, let me get out of your way. I'll have some snacks prepared.'

'Ma, you shouldn't be moving around—'

'You can take your friends to your father's office,' she called back, disappearing into the kitchen. 'The maids will be cleaning downstairs.'

Lucas didn't move, so they all just stood together in the vestibule for a moment, watching Mrs Chan walk away.

'I like your mother,' Alma said. 'She's fun.'

Alma still sounded like Alma, but her cheeks were sunken, her eyes glassy and manic. There were small cuts on the back of her left hand, as though she had been scratching herself, pulling at the skin.

'Are you okay?' Joaquin asked.

She looked at him a moment too long, then nodded. 'I'm fine,' she said. 'I just haven't been sleeping too well.'

'Do you still hear the—' He touched his ear.

Alma nodded. Kept nodding. Hummed along to the music only she could hear.

Sofia turned to Lucas. 'Do you want us to leave?'

Yes, Joaquin thought. *Yes, we want you to leave.*

'Of course, not,' Lucas said. Joaquin glared at him from behind Sofia. 'Let's go upstairs.'

Mr Chan's office was narrow and long, with a tall bookshelf on one wall and a black sofa on the other, his desk flush against the wall opposite the door, the first hulking thing you see in the darkness when you enter, until your knee hit the couch.

'Damn it,' Lucas whispered, rubbing his knee as he switched on the lights. 'This thing always gets me.'

'Cool,' Alma said as she sat on the sofa, her jeans squeaking against the leather, admiring the bookshelf, running a thumb through the sheaf of papers on the low table in front of her. 'I don't think we've ever been in this room.'

'Tita doesn't want two girls in her son's room,' Sofia said.

'You and I have been in his room,' Alma said.

'And so has Lia, but never at the same time.'

'One is the quota.'

Sofia laughed. Joaquin saw a glimpse of that old twinkle in her eye, but he knew it was transient. It broke his heart.

'Just so we're clear,' Lucas said, hands crossed, leaning against his father's bookshelf, 'you cut up your father's face.'

Joaquin sat on the floor by his feet. The girls fell silent, smiles wiped from their faces.

This wasn't the way to speak to someone disturbed, right? Shouldn't you be gentler? 'I haven't seen you two in class,' Joaquin said, earning a disgusted scoff from Lucas. 'Have you left school?'

'I can't sleep,' Alma said, shrugging. 'My mother made me stay home. Have I told you I can't sleep?'

'Yes,' Joaquin said. 'How long has it been going on?'

'There were symbols in my notebook,' Alma replied, playing with her hair. 'Sophie said.'

Joaquin felt Lucas slide down to the floor. They sat shoulder to shoulder, staring at the two girls. Joaquin felt scared, goosebumps rising on his forearms, but didn't say this out loud.

After a moment, he said, 'Al,' raising his voice a little to make her focus.

She was staring up at the ceiling, the bookshelves, the computer monitor on Mr Chan's desk. Anywhere but at Joaquin. She looked as if she was trying hard to hold back her tears. Joaquin thought of the enormous amount of energy she had to expend to pretend she wasn't falling apart.

'I think,' Alma said, still not looking at him, 'I think you need to listen to what Sophie has to say.'

'Have you been to the doctor at all?'

Alma lowered her head. She glared at Joaquin, but he continued pressing, and she couldn't hold it back any longer.

The tears rolled down her cheeks. 'They can't find anything wrong,' she said, trying hard to speak through her sobs. 'They did all these tests and they said everything looks fine. But the music won't stop, and I can't sleep.'

Sofia did not move to comfort her or even look at her. She was staring straight at Lucas.

'Jesus,' Joaquin said. He stood up, bracing himself against Lucas' shoulder, and grabbed a box of tissues from the bookshelf to bring to Alma. 'Don't cry. I'm sorry. It will be okay.'

'No.' She shook her head. A wisp of hair clung to her wet face. 'You need to listen to Sophie.'

He saw an image in a flash, hitting him like a physical slap: his mother stitching a house, forming an image from Xs of thread, telling him to start here.

What was that?

No.

His mother was dead.

It was not his mother.

He looked down at Alma, and it was as if she could see him see this, this revelation. The curious way she looked at him, as if she knew he was in on the plan, as if he now knew everything. 'Do you understand?' she whispered. 'You need to listen to her.'

Lucas was still on the floor. 'Why did you hurt your father like that, Sophie?' he asked. 'Why did you make us come to your house that night? Why did you make us watch?'

Joaquin jumped away from Alma and went back to sitting on the floor next to Lucas. He saw Sofia's face soften as she answered.

'Because I didn't want to be alone,' she said.

It was the first genuine, lucid sentiment they had heard Sofia express in a long time, and it hit Joaquin hard.

He could see on Lucas' face that it affected him too. It was like speaking to a deranged person who had suddenly become coherent.

It didn't last long. 'You know, it made me appreciate Pauline,' Sofia said. 'We weren't that close, and I didn't think much of her. I thought she was a bit aloof, a bit strange. But now I realize how brave she was. She managed to do all that on her own.' She smiled, the proud friend. 'And she succeeded too. Imagine that. Now her father's doing well and her family's safe and she's happy.'

'Why did you do it, Sophie?' Lucas pressed.

She frowned. 'Lia already explained it all to you. Do you need me to repeat what she said?'

'When did she tell us?'

'In the hospital. In the cafeteria.'

'How did you even—' She wasn't even there. 'Somebody told you,' Joaquin continued, desperate to find a logical explanation.

'It told me,' she clarified. 'It told me this too.' Sofia grabbed a sheaf of paper and a pen from the coffee table and started scribbling on the topmost sheet. This went on for a minute or so, during which Joaquin and Lucas just sat in shocked silence. She finished whatever it was she was sketching and threw the sheet towards Lucas. She moved on to the next sketch, scribbled, threw it to him again, and kept going.

Lucas stared at the first sheet of paper she had thrown his way, hands trembling, tears coating his lashes. 'What the hell,' he whispered. Joaquin grabbed another sheet that had fallen to the floor.

It was a near-exact replica of one of Mrs Chan's CT scans, only this one was rendered in blue ballpoint ink. A map of the tumours in her lungs, patterns of bright light, the malignant circles where they had seen them on the scans that Lucas and Joaquin had shoved back into the envelope, which Lucas had delivered to his parents' room, where it now sat inside the drawer of his father's bedside table, unseen by anyone else.

'What else do you need to see,' Sofia said, 'to believe that this is all real, that this is really happening?'

Joaquin grabbed the pieces of paper from the floor and snatched the sheet from Lucas' hands. 'Lucas, get up,' he said, but he wouldn't budge. Joaquin hooked an arm under his armpit and pulled him up. 'Come on.'

'How did you,' Lucas started to say. 'How is this possible?'

'I think you should leave now,' Joaquin said, holding Lucas steady. 'Lia's on her way and I don't think she wants to see you.'

'How is this possible?' Lucas demanded.

'You need to be present for the next stage so I can save all of you,' Sofia said.

'What do you mean?'

Joaquin wished he could stop Lucas from talking, from engaging with this. 'Sophie,' he said, more furious now than scared. 'Will you just go?'

'If you don't come with me, your mother will suffer, and then she will die,' Sofia told Lucas. 'You know that, right?' She then pointed at herself, 'I will be sick, and I will never recover.'

'You don't know that,' Joaquin said, dragged back into this insane web against his will.

'Lia's parents will be in a horrible accident.'

'You don't know any of that. You can't possibly know any of that.'

'And your father will kill you,' Sofia said to Joaquin, 'or you will kill your father. One or the other, nothing else.'

Joaquin began to drag Lucas out of the room.

Sofia stood up, the sheaf of papers falling from her lap to the floor, exploding like so many white petals. 'It already visited you last night,' she said. 'You know what I'm talking about. Everything is going to be okay if you just come to the house with me.'

'You know what you can do?' Joaquin said. 'You can stop talking about it. Find help. You're disturbed.'

'I got lost on my way home and now I'm standing on a landmine with all of my friends,' Sofia said. 'What do you want me to do now? Even if I ignore what's happening, the landmine will still detonate. There's no turning back now.'

'Go to hell, Sophie,' Joaquin said, and slammed the door behind him.

When Emilia arrived, Sofia and Alma had already gone, sneaking out before the snacks came, a maid carrying a tray of spring rolls and glasses of fruit juice finding Mr Chan's office empty, pens and papers all over the floor, a box of tissues left tipped on its side on the sofa.

Emilia, Joaquin, and Lucas retreated to Lucas' room. Lucas sat on the edge of his bed while Emilia and Joaquin sat on chairs by his study desk, watching him closely.

'My knight in shining armour,' Emilia said, in the hopes of clearing away the dark cloud that now hung over Lucas. 'How's your wrist?'

He didn't answer.

Joaquin began to talk, like a criminal confessing to a priest that he hoped could absolve him. He took out Sofia's sketches from his back pocket and handed them to Emilia, twisting Lucas' gooseneck lamp to shine more light on the page. She ran her fingers across them, touching the grooves left by the ballpoint pen, the sure lines drawn with no hesitation.

'She knew everything,' Lucas said, gesturing towards the sketches in her hands. 'She sketched the scans to the tiniest detail. The scans that she never saw. How could she know all that?'

Beneath the horror of the situation, she felt a profound helplessness. On the phone, when Joaquin said the tumours were 'everywhere', she didn't quite visualize precisely what *everywhere* meant.

'I'm so sorry, Lucas,' Emilia said. 'I'm so sorry.' It was all she could say.

'She said your parents will be in an accident,' Joaquin said.

Emilia twisted the sheets of paper in her hands. 'An accident?' she repeated. 'And what did she say about Alma?'

'What? I don't know. I'm sure she said something. She said she needed to save all of us.'

Lucas covered his face with his hands. Emilia and Joaquin sat in silence for several minutes, listening to him weep. Then Lucas lowered his hands, sniffed, and wiped his eyes with the back of his arm.

'How's your wrist?' Emilia asked, trying to be a good friend again.

Lucas smiled at her. 'I'm okay, considering.'

They shared a laugh, and everything felt almost normal. But then he said, 'What if it's true?'

'What?'

'Sophie talks like everything would be resolved if we just followed her to the house. What if it's true?'

'You're not thinking straight,' Joaquin said.

'You shouldn't have let her come here,' Emilia said. 'Now she's infected you too.'

'There was something in my room last night,' Lucas said.

Emilia felt her breath hitch in shock. An image of Miss Cardenas crouching on the side of her bed, a black goat embracing her from behind. The smell of soil and rot and sweet perfume. *What is the divine but that which is beyond understanding or explanation?*

'What do you mean?' Joaquin asked, but Lucas wouldn't say.

'I know you think the story I told you is crazy,' Emilia said. 'But let me ask you this: would you kill someone to save your mother?'

'Wouldn't you?' he shot back.

Emilia shook her head. 'You don't know what you're saying.'

'I beat up that butcher,' Lucas said. 'I never thought I was violent. I never thought I could hurt someone like that, but I did. It felt easy. It even felt good. Don't look at me like that.' This was directed to Joaquin, who seemed ready to hit something right now. 'Didn't you say he deserved it?'

'I didn't know you enjoyed hurting people,' Joaquin said.

This seemed to sting Lucas. 'Come on. I didn't mean it like that.'

'Then what did you mean? That beating someone up felt good, but you're not like my father?'

Emilia wished they would just punch each other right now. At least then she would know when to step in, when to pull them apart. See where the blows were coming from, where they were landing.

'Sophie said it's either your father will kill you, or you will kill him,' Lucas said. 'Guess what I think would most likely happen?'

Joaquin looked away.

'And you, Lia, your parents will get hurt. If I could stop all that by killing someone, I would. Wouldn't you?'

He would tell Emilia all this again at the hospital, with both of her parents in the ICU, like he was waiting for her to tell him that they were right to decide to go through with it, and that she was wrong.

Oh, no. She would not give him that satisfaction.

He could lie to himself, rewrite what happened to make it seem like they had no choice, that their hands were tied.

Of course, they had a choice. Of course, they did. Didn't she choose this too?

'What if it wasn't true?' Emilia said now, sitting in Lucas' room, the window above his headboard turning into a dark square as evening fell. 'What if it were all lies? I know I told you that Pauline did it all and was rewarded, but what if you kill someone and everything horrible that was supposed to happen still happened? What then?'

Lucas looked exhausted. Emilia couldn't blame him, she felt about ready to pass out.

He didn't respond to the question, but instead, fidgeting with the Velcro on his wrist brace, said, 'You better get ready if you're staying for dinner, Lia. I think Ma's already setting the table.'

Emilia couldn't stay for dinner. She didn't want to. Joaquin had snuck her in earlier; Mrs Chan didn't even know she was there, didn't even know Sofia and Alma had already left. Mrs Chan was probably setting the table now for three guests, adding pink flowers to her crystal centrepiece for her son's visitors.

Emilia waited for Mrs Chan to walk back into the kitchen before rushing out the door with Joaquin, the better to avoid any more gracious offers of hospitality that she would have to decline.

'Are you sure you don't want me to walk you back home?' Joaquin asked.

Dusk was fast approaching, turning the sky a delicate violet. They stood outside the gate, enveloped by the sweet scent of the Chans' blooming sampaguita.

'And make you miss dinner?'

Joaquin sighed deeply. He placed his hands in his pockets, bounced on the balls of his feet. The Chans' house glowed a brilliant yellow in the growing darkness. 'I think I want to miss it, at this point.'

'I would invite you over, but you know that won't go over well with my parents.'

He smiled.

'Lucas cares about you,' she said.

Joaquin looked down at the ground and shook his head. 'Do you think you could ever kill someone?'

Emilia sighed.

'Lucas sounded so sure,' he said.

She kicked at the soil, drew a circle with her sneaker. 'Everything seems easy when you're just talking hypothetically.'

'So you don't think you could ever kill someone.'

She frowned at him. 'No. And I don't think you could do something like that too.'

He didn't seem convinced.

'Joaquin, you need to keep an eye on him.'

'I know, I know,' he said. 'Should I just tackle Sophie to the ground when she shows up again?'

They chuckled.

'You know what's terrible?' Joaquin said.

'What?'

'When I heard that his mother's dying, one of my first thoughts was, now I can't ask Mr Chan for a loan.'

They said nothing for a while.

'It's normal to think that,' Emilia said.

'Is it?' He looked as if he were in pain.

'It's normal to be a little selfish,' she said. 'It's hard, with your father being—' How could she describe him? Words failed her. 'You want life to be just a bit easier. It's normal to want that. It's not too much to ask.'

Joaquin gave her a look, and Emilia suddenly felt a bit embarrassed. She had said too much.

'Did Sophie say anything about my father being sick?' she asked.

'No,' he said. 'Wait. Is your father sick?'

'I don't know. But now you're telling me that Sophie said my parents might end up in an accident. So I guess I should worry about that instead.'

'What's happening with your father?'

Emilia didn't reply. If she said nothing, thought it was nothing, it would go away on its own.

'It's okay,' she said. 'Don't worry about it.'

Joaquin looked like he wanted to ask more questions, but he didn't press her. 'Thanks for coming,' he said.

'I don't know if I even helped.'

He shrugged. 'It helps to know I'm not losing my mind. Text me when you're home?'

She nodded, shooed him away from the gate. 'Go sit down for dinner.'

When Emilia got home, she found her mother kneeling in front of the table that held their TV in the living room. She was going through the boxes of papers in the drawers. 'Your dinner is in the kitchen, anak,' her mother said without looking up.

'Have you eaten?' She sat on the sofa in front of the TV, watching her mother sift through what looked like old receipts.

'I have, but your father has no appetite. He's sleeping now. If you're going to watch TV, you need to lower the volume.'

'How can I even watch TV when you're in the way?'

Her parents were strict, hardworking, reserved—affable enough to laugh at her jokes and pretend-insolence, but not warm enough for them to be the first people she would think to run to for comfort. They had clothed and fed her and, unlike some of her friends' parents, never physically hurt her, but whenever she thought back to the rare times when she sought advice or consolation, she could only remember moments that cut deep and, to her surprise and shame, continued to sting in the years that followed. Her mother throwing her report card at her face after receiving less than stellar grades. Her father laughing at her as she cried over a bleeding cut on her arm, *It's just a scratch, stop your bellyaching*. Their snide comments when she froze on stage during an elementary school play—*You can't stop talking at home, and now, all of a sudden, when you really need to talk, you forget to open your mouth*.

There would always be that distance. She could never be completely vulnerable around them the way she was around her friends, knowing that ridicule and contempt was just around the corner from her parents' love. Did they feel this way about her too? Did they see her as a trap door poised to fall? She had often wondered. Perhaps they looked at her and saw only a disappointing, inexplicable stranger.

They knew nothing about what was happening with Sofia, and they never would.

Her mother had stopped rifling through the papers. She was staring at her. Emilia could tell, by the way her mother's head was tilted, that she had asked her a question that she didn't hear.

'Did you say something?'

Her mother sighed. 'Do you know how to apply for a passport?'

Emilia didn't expect this answer. 'A passport?'

'Lydia said—you remember Lydia, the one who owns the stall next to ours?'

'The one who sells vegetables?'

Her mother nodded and gathered the papers she had plucked from the boxes. She stood up with a soft grunt and sat on the sofa next to her. 'She went to Singapore with her husband. She said fares can be very cheap when they go on sale. You can buy them online. Do you know how to do that?'

'Sure.' Emilia took out her phone. Using 3G would eat up her credits, but she didn't have a PC or Wi-Fi connection at home, and she wanted to help her mother. She opened a browser tab and navigated to Philippine Airlines' website. Her mother moved closer and peered over her shoulder at the tiny screen of her Nokia. SEAT SALE, the screen screamed once the page loaded.

'Hmm,' her mother said. 'Look at that.' She nodded with approval. 'But first, we need a passport.'

'You want to go to Singapore?' They had never flown overseas. Emilia and her father had never even set foot on a plane before. Her mother had, but the only time she had flown was ten years ago, when Emilia's grandfather suddenly died and her mother had to rush home to Isabela, the province where she was born, to be present at the burial.

'It doesn't have to be Singapore,' her mother said as Emilia looked up passport document requirements on her phone. 'Your father always wanted to go abroad for vacation.'

Her father, who couldn't even eat, whom she had seen writhe in pain in bed, muffling a scream, her mother shooing her away, not to worry, the doctors were on top of things.

'Lydia keeps talking about how easy it is,' her mother went on, 'and how we can travel for cheap. We just need to be smart.'

Emilia realized that her parents had never before expressed to her a want, a dream, or even a simple wish for their own future, and the weight of it suddenly felt unnatural and oppressive, like a storm she was powerless to stop.

'Okay,' Emilia said now, reading a list from a government website, 'you need to set an appointment online and appear in person at a passport service site.'

'Is there one nearby?'

'There should be one in Bulacan,' she responded. 'We can check later. At your appointment, you need to bring original copies and photocopies of your birth certificate, marriage contract, and another government ID.' She tilted the screen towards her mother. 'They have a whole list of IDs that they accept. You have a postal ID, don't you?'

'We have those documents that they need,' her mother said, lifting the sheaf of papers in her hands.

'You shouldn't have these just lying around downstairs. What if it floods?' The papers smelled like the old shirts Emilia had that had been stuck for years in her closet, dotted with ancient moth balls. She looked through the documents. CERTIFICATE OF LIVE BIRTH, one read, the letters hardly legible. 'You can't bring these, though.'

Her mother frowned. 'Why not?'

'You need to bring copies certified by the NSO.'

'But these are originals.'

'Yes, but the NSO-certified ones are what they want. Look.' She showed the webpage again. 'You can apply for copies online.'

'I need to apply for copies of a document that I already have.'

Emilia had to laugh. 'Yes, and it would look exactly like that, just printed on their own paper. And you need to pay for it.'

'That's outrageous.'

Her mother took the papers back and idly shuffled through them on her lap. Emilia wasn't laughing any more. It felt as if she was walking with her mother down a road that was new and pretty and pleasant, and now, all of a sudden, there was nowhere left to turn, nowhere left to go.

'I heard it's hard to get passport appointments,' Emilia said. 'But we can book one now. We can do all of these things online right now. Order your NSO documents, choose a date and a passport service site.'

But her mother had already turned away, already drawn the curtain in front of a dream she had been staring at for who knew how long. 'You need to appear in person, though, don't you?'

'You do, Nanay.'

'Your father is sick, and I can't close the store.'

'Not even for one day?' Emilia said. 'You can have the NSO documents delivered. You don't even need to pick them up. You just need to appear in person for the appointment so they can take your photo.'

Her mother stood up. 'I'll think about it *muna*, anak.' Even though Emilia knew she wouldn't. 'Maybe when your father gets better, so we can go to the same appointment.'

Why did she feel that her father would never get better?

A faint call from the doorway as her mother walked to the bedroom: 'Wash the dishes after you eat.'

Emilia lifted the lid from the pot in the kitchen, stared at the pork and potatoes and pig liver swimming in sauce. Her mother had prepared menudo, her father's favourite—that he wasn't even able to eat.

In the middle of the table was a rotting banana, a small container of fish sauce, and today's lunch leftovers—half a fried fish, sauteed kangkong—under a plastic lid. Emilia got herself a small scoop of rice, some meat and sauce, a glass of water. She picked at the fried fish now sitting gummy and limp on its plate. She sat at the table for her solitary dinner, looked up at the large image of Mary and the baby Christ looming over her from the wall, and began to cry.

'Don't tell me you don't like menudo.'

Emilia jumped, covered her mouth to suppress a startled scream.

Miss Cardenas sat across from her, hands folded on top of the table. She placed a finger over her lips. *Shh*. 'You wouldn't want to wake your father.'

After that initial shock, Emilia's heartbeat began to slow. She didn't move to bolt out of the room. She continued to cry, but not out of terror. A simple continuation of her mourning. Was she asleep? Was she dreaming? Was this a reality she was now happy to accept? What did it matter now? Miss Cardenas looked surprised and delighted.

'You see?' her dead teacher said, arms outstretched across the table, as though to hold her hands. 'It's like we're old friends.'

If she didn't acknowledge it, it would go away. But it didn't seem to be going away, the dread sitting right next to her, walking with her everywhere. 'My father is dying, isn't he?' Emilia said.

Miss Cardenas withdrew her arms from reach, folded her hands again, like a doctor bringing her grim news. But she was still smiling.

'And my mother knows,' Emilia said. 'That's why she wants to go on vacation with him. But there might not even be enough time left.'

'Those pesky passport appointments,' Miss Cardenas said. 'So hard to come by. Everyone just wants to leave.'

'So it's true?' Emilia's tears pooled at her chin. She wiped them away with the back of her hand.

Miss Cardenas tilted her head. A menacing wink. 'So now you believe me?'

Emilia kept silent, her head filled with static, thoughts rumbling around and whizzing by so fast that she couldn't catch one quick enough to understand.

'Isn't it sad,' Miss Cardenas said, 'how some people work hard all their life, and then they just die without even enjoying a moment of the fruits of their hard labour?'

For a split-second, Emilia could pretend that she was indeed talking to her teacher, who was not dead, whose face was not being worn by something else. 'I don't know what to do,' she said.

The response was swift. 'Of course, you know what to do, my darling.'

Emilia pushed her plate of food away. She watched Miss Cardenas watch this with an eager look on her face.

'You don't even need to do much,' Miss Cardenas said, leaning across the table. 'Your friend has done all the hard work. You just need to be there. Participate.'

'How do I know you're real?' Emilia said.

A gleeful laugh. How many times had she seen Miss Cardenas look exactly like this—eyes wide, hands over her mouth, a tiny shriek—after someone cracked a joke in class, or a fellow teacher whispered a piece of raunchy gossip. *I can't believe you just said that.*

'I think I know what you mean, but please—' Miss Cardenas now with her hands open, palms up on the table, '—elaborate.'

Emilia knew it would be like stepping into a furious river, and yet she pushed forward. 'How do I know that what we'll ask of you will actually happen?' she said. Bargaining like Peter looking for the holes in the resurrected form, when whoever's wearing Miss Cardenas wanted her to be perhaps like Job, or Abraham. Ever-patient, ever-obedient, bearing down upon a living, breathing body against the stone altar without question, without hesitation.

'Is that what you want?' Miss Cardenas said. 'Some proof?'

'What if you lie?'

'What happened to Pauline is not enough proof?'

'How can I trust you?' Emilia sobbed. 'What happened to Pauline may not happen to me.'

'So you want what Pauline got. Even though you know what Pauline did.' Miss Cardenas smiled. 'What is it that you want, my sweet? I need to hear you say it.'

'I want my father to get better,' she said.

'You want what everyone wants,' Miss Cardenas replied. 'A good life. A happy life. An easy life. I can give you a taste of it tomorrow. But just for tomorrow. That would be your proof.'

Emilia cried.

'Say yes,' Miss Cardenas said.

Here now, the water that would sweep her away.

'Yes,' Emilia mumbled into the sofa, waking up, her phone still in her hand. She pushed herself up, walked to the kitchen, saw the pot of menudo beneath the lid. The house felt cold, as though it had been raining outside, but there was no rain.

Her father was up early the next day. Emilia, who couldn't sleep a wink, found him in the kitchen, whistling a happy melody, heating up last night's menudo on the stove.

'Are you feeling better?' she asked, and the way he said, 'Yes', so joyful and succinct, hurt her like a sudden flash of bright light.

'No more pain,' he said with a smile, patting his belly. 'I'm even going to the store today.'

'But we're still going to the doctor at some point,' said her mother, who had entered the kitchen. 'Just to see what's going on.'

'Of course, of course,' her father said, stirring the menudo. 'But I'm really feeling good. It's miraculous.'

Her mother turned to her, lowered her voice, 'You order our NSO documents, okay, anak?'

'Oh,' Emilia said, tasting the bile climbing up her throat. 'Okay. Sure. I can do that.'

'Do you want breakfast, Lia?' her father said, squinting at them. 'What are you two talking about?'

'I don't want breakfast,' Emilia said. 'I think I'll try to go back to sleep.'

Is that what you want? Some proof?

I can give you a taste of it tomorrow.

She returned to her bedroom but all she could do was sit on her bed and stare at the wall for hours, terrified to go to sleep, terrified to once again see not-Miss Cardenas and that gleeful, eager, hungry smile: *It's like we're old friends.*

A sharp, audible intake of breath, and Emilia was in the house, seeing the look of shock and horror on Miss Cardenas' face before Pauline pulled her by the arm deeper into the house and stuck a knife in her throat. Once. Twice.

A millisecond of silence, then Miss Cardenas hit the floor, and it was as if this movement was a floodgate that opened and now allowed all sound to come rushing in: Pauline screaming in terror, shoes scratching on the floorboards, Miss Cardenas choking, a gurgling sound like a drainpipe. Emilia felt herself leaving her body, silence flowed in like water—peace, finally, peace—but the sound came back, and it was Pauline screaming—

'Oh my God,' she could hear her saying. 'Oh my God, oh my God.'

The mannequin sat on the chair, elbows on knees, leaning forward, its veil nearly brushing Miss Cardenas, who lay gasping on her side by the mannequin's feet, her fingers trying to reach the knife in her throat. Pauline stopped screaming. She braced herself against the teacher's shoulder and pulled the knife out. Miss Cardenas' hands and feet twitching, twitching, the blood gushing out of her mouth and out of the wound in her throat in pulses.

The movements growing smaller and smaller with each passing second.

Emilia could hear someone moaning in disgust and in sorrow and in anger, and realized that the sound was coming from deep in her throat. The smell of blood in the humid air. She couldn't jump across the chasm created by the minutes between the Miss Cardenas who was being dragged into the room and the Miss Cardenas who now lay before her, whose smell was making her gag.

A fatal wound and you go from a person to a piece of meat. How could it be that easy? It shouldn't be this easy.

Emilia jerked awake. She slapped her cheeks. No, no.

But what was that thought bubbling up just now?

It could be that easy.

When she closed her eyes and fell into a dream again, she was outside Pauline's home, helping her friend feed the chickens. Pauline reached into her bowl and threw cracked corn to the ground. The feed in Emilia's bowl didn't feel like corn. The texture made her uneasy. 'What kind of poultry feed is this?' Emilia asked, reaching into her bowl, and grabbing a handful of bloody teeth.

Part III

Ascension

Sofia insisted that she would do the dishes, but all she did was dump the plates in the sink and slink out of the kitchen. They heard a door close, perhaps the door to her bedroom. Without a word, Lucas and Joaquin rose from the table and stood side by side in front of the sink, Lucas firing up another cigarette, washing up while Joaquin wiped the dishes using an old rag. The rain fell harder, a constant drumming on the rooftops. Joaquin took a scratched plastic mug from a cupboard and placed it on the floor to catch the rainwater. Every action smooth and easy. Just another routine task, like the pill box, as though they had been doing this for years, which they must have been.

Lucas noticed Emilia looking and said, 'Go on, you girls get some rest.'

'How chivalrous,' Michelle said with a sly smile, patting his arm. The bewildered look Joaquin threw Lucas made Michelle snicker.

There was a dead moth in one corner of the guest room, next to where Lucas or Joaquin had left a rolled-up mat. Emilia attempted to kick it away, but the moth's wings instantly turned to dust. She felt goosebumps rise on her arms. She didn't want to think of how long the moth had lain there.

She unrolled the mat and placed a thin mattress on top of it, while Michelle fluffed up the pillows on the bed.

'Take the bed,' Michelle said.

'No, you take it. I'm okay here.' She lay on top of the mattress on the floor and stared at the ceiling. The room had beige walls with chocolate-brown trim, and the ceiling was white. Or rather, it was white a long time ago. Now it was white with rust-coloured water stains, the paint wrinkling and ballooning in some places. Big cobwebs filled the corners.

She focused on a movement in one of the webs. Fluttering wings. Another moth, about to die.

'We can share the bed if the floor's too cold.' The springs squeaked as Michelle tried to find a comfortable position. 'What was that all about?'

Emilia wasn't sure what she was referring to.

'What you said earlier. Folly something.'

Ah.

'Folie à deux,' Emilia said. '"The madness of two". It's just something we've talked about before. Shared psychosis. A hallucination shared by two people who live in close proximity. There was a famous case. In New Zealand. Two girls, Pauline and Juliet, became close friends, created elaborate fantasies, and acted out their stories. They believed in a place called the Fourth World, a place only they and a few chosen others could see. It sounds completely crazy, but these girls believed it was real.' She cleared her throat. 'There was a movie about it, with Kate Winslet?'

'Ooh,' Michelle said, typing on her phone, searching online. 'I bet it didn't end well?'

'They conspired to kill Pauline's mother.'

'No way.' A pause. '"Folie à Deux" is also a studio album by Fall Out Boy.'

Emilia laughed. What else was there to do? The rain and the darkness felt oppressive. Claustrophobic.

'Then what did Sofia say?' Michelle asked.

'Folie à plusieurs,' Emilia responded. 'The madness of many.'

'You guys are super intense,' Michelle said. 'I don't mean to pry, and you don't need to explain anything, but it really feels like something big happened in the past.'

'Sorry,' was all Emilia could say.

'You're not,' Michelle began to say, 'you're not serial killers, are you?'

Emilia burst out laughing. Michelle peeked over the edge of her bed, smiling at her.

'Just trying to lighten the mood.' Michelle winked at her, and Emilia felt pain deep within her gut. 'Get some rest.'

Michelle turned to her side after a moment and fell asleep almost instantly, softly snoring. Emilia stood up, careful not to make a noise. Michelle fell asleep cradling her phone. Emilia stepped out of the room.

Lucas was sitting by the front door, smoking, watching the rain. He smiled when he saw her approach. She grabbed another chair and sat next to him. They were getting sprayed by the rain, the chilly breeze making her shiver, but she stayed put, sitting next to him in silence. Lucas blew cigarette smoke up to the sky.

'You never smoked while we were in high school,' Emilia said, and wondered if she was making a mistake, bringing their high school years into this conversation.

He shook his head. 'My father smoked. I started doing it as SCC.' He smirked. 'I guess teaching drives you to ruin.'

'But you enjoy it? Teaching?'

'Let's say I enjoy smoking more.'

'Come on.'

She grabbed a random notebook from one of the boxes and opened it to a page with words written in Latin.

Sors immanis
et inanis,
rota tu volubilis,
status malus,
vana salus
semper dissolubilis

'Did Sofia write this?' Emilia asked, tilting the page towards Lucas so he could see.

'That's her handwriting,' he said, 'but that's from a medieval poem. "O Fortuna".'

Emilia was both surprised and unsurprised when Lucas began reciting the translation of the passage from memory: 'Fate—monstrous and empty, you whirling wheel, you are malevolent, well-being is vain and always fades to nothing.'

She closed the notebook, suddenly remembering Sofia pointing at a blank page and screaming at the top of her lungs.

'It was set to music by a German composer,' Lucas said. 'Then it was used in a Rogin-E commercial.'

Emilia laughed. 'I remember that. Wow.'

Lucas smiled at her, sighed deeply as his smile faded. 'Everything I know,' he said, 'it's all just worthless trivia. It doesn't matter. It didn't matter. It didn't help anyone or make one bit of difference.'

Emilia stayed silent, feeling the edges of a dangerous discussion approaching.

'And the money.' He shook his head. 'Growing up, I knew I was richer than the other children around me. I didn't think it was strange or unfair. I just accepted it as a fact of life. It made me think that, somehow, my family was better compared to everyone else's. That I was better.' He scoffed and shook his head. 'I'm an idiot. When I first saw the bruise on Joaquin's face, I thought I could save him. And Sophie. And Alma. And you, especially after what happened to your parents. I thought I could save you all, with the things I know. Or failing that, at least with my money. My parents' money. Then the money dried up, and it turns out I couldn't save anyone after all.'

She leaned against his shoulder. 'Goddamn it,' she heard him whisper to himself, wiping tears from his eyes.

'Remember that butcher you beat up?' Emilia said, staying in her position, wrapping her arms around his arm. His shoulders shook as he laughed. 'Do you tell your students that? That you once beat up a guy so hard you sent him to the emergency room? Over a girl?'

'How chivalrous,' Lucas said, imitating Michelle, making her double over, laughing.

After recovering from her laughter, she said, 'It's not all worthless.'

He looked at her.

'You're a teacher. You're helping people. That means something.'

'Sure,' he said. 'Whatever.'

'You must be popular with students,' she said, teasing. 'Young teacher like you.'

'Like Miss Cardenas?' he said.

Silence.

Emilia inched away, moving her chair away from him as if he suddenly repulsed her.

'I want to go home,' she said. She didn't know which home she meant. Not her apartment in the city. Not her family home not that far from here, now with a new family living in it, the house sold to them to help her pay for her parents' medical expenses. To help her leave and live. Not this house, nor this time, but a home in the past, the floorboards in Lucas' room reflecting the sunlight, their group of friends eating junk food and walking home together as they planned their futures. But nothing could turn back time. Pauline even asked. The answer would always be no.

Fate, monstrous and empty.

'This stupid rain and this stupid car,' Emilia said. Lucas flicked away the remains of his cigarette, the ember extinguished instantly by the puddle forming beyond the porch.

'Lia,' Lucas said.

The heavy, urgent way he said her name made her look at him.

'About the car—'

'There you are.'

Joaquin was standing behind them, holding up a bottle of cheap whisky. 'Found this in the kitchen.'

'Nice,' Lucas said. He nudged Emilia gently with his elbow. 'You should grab Michelle.'

'You were going to say something about the car,' she said.

'Oh,' he said, brushing cigarette ash off his shirt front. 'I was just about to say I'm sorry that happened. I knew you didn't want to be here.'

'But we're glad you're here,' Joaquin said, holding the bottle of whisky like a trophy. 'Right, Lucas? Play nice.'

Lucas struck a dramatic pose, hand on his heart, and fake-affronted, 'We were just reminiscing about old times. Like that butcher I punched.'

'Oh, right. Your greatest accomplishment.'

Emilia stood up, fake laughing, because *Like Miss Cardenas?* was still echoing in her head, because Lucas looked as if he wanted to tell her something else. About the car. Something.

Joaquin took her seat, placed the bottle of whisky on the floor, and joined Lucas in staring at the rain.

Whatever it was that Lucas wanted to say, he didn't want to say it in front of Joaquin, for some reason. 'Let me go get Michelle,' she said, and left.

Michelle was sitting up in bed when Emilia entered the room, as though she had been waiting for her.

'You're awake,' Emilia said. They smiled at each other. 'Joaquin found a—'

'You like her, don't you?'

Emilia narrowed her eyes, the smile still on her face as she tried to understand what she was saying. *What?* Michelle's hands folded on the pillow on her lap, her phone beside her. Wide smile, a knowing wink. Michelle continued to smile even as Emilia's knees buckled, finally understanding that this was no longer Michelle.

'You didn't tell Michelle the whole story,' not-Michelle continued, 'because you didn't want her to think less of you. She's a fresh start, a new friend, who could help you recreate yourself. But then you brought her here. Why did you bring her here?'

Emilia started to cry.

Michelle tilted her head, clucked her tongue. 'Oh, darling. You shouldn't be ashamed. You just want to be desired. Everyone wants to be desired. But you're too broken to allow anyone to come close. You understand that, don't you?' Michelle lay on her stomach and slid towards the edge of the bed, cupping her chin. 'There was that one boy in college, right? It lasted for a couple of years, but in the end, he couldn't stand you too. Whenever he would fall silent, or look away, you'd immediately think you did something wrong. "Are you mad at me? Are you mad at me? What did I do? Tell me, please." Saying sorry over and over for every little slight. "Sorry I bumped into you when I was tossing in bed. Sorry I took a bite of my dinner while waiting for you to finish your call. Sorry I left a dirty mug in the sink." Even when he said there was nothing you needed to apologize for. That he didn't expect you to be perfect, because no one is perfect. That he loved you just as you are. But you were deaf to all that. You remained hypervigilant, like an animal constantly sensing a predator. You needed constant reassurance because you couldn't believe he would want to be with you. He got so sick of it. He wanted a partner, not a goddamn glass bowl he needed to balance on top of his head.

'You were like that with every person who tried to open up a space in their life to let you in, and no one stuck around. Remember film class, when you joined a group to watch a film for extra credit? You were so excited to talk to them about it afterwards, but no one wanted to talk to you, they talked among themselves. They were the chill, cool kids on campus and they found you needy and anxious and strange. The cold, empty stare they gave you and the giddy enthusiasm they had when they turned away from you to talk to one another, that cut you deep. You still remember that. What did you learn?'

She couldn't help but respond to her. 'I don't belong anywhere.'

'And?'

'No one wants me,' Emilia said, 'I'm meant to be alone.'

A deep, satisfied sigh from Michelle. 'Yes. You are just this broken thing that unfortunately needs to continue existing, a jagged piece going through the world and cutting up everything beautiful into shreds. So you stopped trying to connect with other people, tried to befriend your own isolation. Alma felt the same way, you know. For years and years and years and years—'

'Stop it.'

'Imagine how lonely she must have felt.'

Emilia cried. 'I said, stop it.'

'And then,' Michelle said, looking amused, 'after twelve years, you decide to make a new friend. And you bring her here. Why did you bring her here?'

Emilia turned her head and found herself lying on her side, on the bed next to Michelle, facing her. Michelle was fast asleep. She stirred a few seconds later, still cradling her phone, and rubbed her right eye. 'Em?'

'I'm sorry,' Emilia said, jumping away from her. 'I don't know how I got here.'

'That's okay. Stay on the bed. I told you the floor is too cold.'

When did waking end and the nightmare begin? 'I think Joaquin found some whisky,' she said. 'Would you like to go the living room? They want to have a drink.'

Michelle's face broke into a wide smile that unsettled Emilia. *But you're too broken to allow anyone to come close. You understand that, don't you?* 'Nice. Shall we?'

Joaquin approached them the moment they emerged in the living room, handing them their glasses right away. Whisky, a splash of Coke, couple of ice cubes. On the coffee table were a bowl of leftovers from their caldereta and bags of snacks they had scrounged from the kitchen. Salted peanuts, watermelon seeds, potato chips. Michelle grabbed a handful of nuts and began to eat before knocking back her drink in three hungry gulps.

'Whoa,' Emilia said.

Michelle giggled. 'Sorry. It's been a long day.' Joaquin topped up her glass with more whisky.

They sat where they had sat that afternoon, when they first spoke to Sofia in this room, as though they were given designated seats on a doomed flight: Lucas and Joaquin on chairs next to each other, Emilia and Michelle sitting together on the sofa, Sofia on the chair facing them.

Lucas blasted pop music on his phone—'Do you like Taylor Swift?' Michelle demanded—while Sofia worked through a mound of watermelon seeds, smiling to herself. The festive atmosphere did little to lift Emilia's spirits. She leaned forward to speak to Lucas. 'Were we talking earlier today?'

He looked up from his phone. 'What do you mean?'

'About—' What was it about? '—the Rogin-E commercial?'

He frowned, then laughed. 'That was just a few minutes ago, Lia. Yes, we were sitting by the door.' He paused, and then asked, 'Are you all right?'

She took a sip of her drink. 'I thought I dreamt it.'

'Did you ever get a priest out there?' Michelle said.

She asked the question as if she were leaping into an existing conversation, but everyone else looked confused. 'Out where?' Lucas asked.

'The house,' she said. 'The weird house that we saw on our way here.' She waved her hands about, trying to explain. 'You know. To bless it. If it really were haunted.'

'We did, actually,' Joaquin said.

This was news to Emilia. 'You did?'

He nodded. 'Lucas and I did. The priest was patient enough to listen to a couple of teenagers. But he had a heart attack on the way there.'

'No way,' Michelle said.

'Why do you ask?' Lucas said. 'You're still thinking about the house?'

Michelle shrugged. 'I was just curious.'

The group then fell into a silence that felt dangerous to Emilia, like the quiet before a storm hits. Joaquin, tapping a hand on his knee in time with the music, said, 'Don't you miss this, Lia?'

Michelle looked at him and scoffed. Emilia homed in on this insolence powered by too much whisky, wondering what Michelle would say next.

'What?' Joaquin said, guarded.

'You keep giving her hell for not wanting to come back here,' Michelle said. 'But honestly? If both of my parents were dead, I wouldn't want to return to my hometown too.'

Everyone stopped moving, save for Michelle, who gulped another mouthful of whisky and Coke.

Lucas and Joaquin spoke almost at the same time:

'Who told you that?'

'Lia's parents aren't dead.'

Emilia's fingers squeaked against the glass she was holding on her lap.

'Have they,' Lucas began to say, leaning forward to catch her attention, 'Are they dead, Lia? Did something happen?'

Everyone looked at her, silent and waiting.

She drank her whisky instead of answering. Lucas sat back and crossed his arms.

'What?' Michelle said.

'They're in Isabela, up north, where Lia's mother was originally from,' Joaquin explained, throwing glances at Emilia, who said nothing. 'Her father got sick for a while, and they were in a terrible bus accident, but they're both still alive.'

Emilia felt tears burning in the corner of her eyes. She took another sip of her drink, her hand shaking.

'Why would you tell me your parents are dead?' Michelle asked.

'I—' What could she say? No one was jumping in to help her respond. 'I don't know, I don't talk to them any more—'

'Why not?' Michelle's tone had become gentler.

'I need them to stay away.'

'From here?'

'And from me.'

Michelle frowned, an edge returning to her tone. 'I don't get it.'

'It's hard to explain. They're safer where they are.'

'But you do understand it's a bit fucked up to tell someone your parents are dead when they're not, right?'

'I—'

'It's just so weird,' Michelle said, and turned away to get another drink from Joaquin. 'Who does that?'

'Maybe I should just go back to the room,' Emilia whispered.

'No,' Sofia said. 'Stay. Finish your drink.'

A moment later and Michelle was lying sideways on the sofa, in deep sleep.

'Wow,' Joaquin said. 'I didn't take her for a lightweight.'

'She drank so fast, though,' Lucas said, lifting the glass from Michelle's hand before it could tumble over and spill its contents. He left the glass on the floor, by his feet.

'You didn't tell me you asked for help from a priest.' Emilia asked.

Lucas shrugged. 'Not much help, in the end.'

'He said it was a house not made with human hands,' Joaquin said.

'But in Corinthians, that's in reference to the eternal home, the one in heaven. So we're still confused what he meant by that. Did he mean that the house was good, or bad?'

'Or neither,' Joaquin said.

'In premodern philosophy,' Lucas began.

'Oh, here we go.'

Lucas punched his shoulder lightly before continuing, 'In premodern philosophy, evil is considered a punishment from God due to the fall of Man. In November 1755, a big part of the city of Lisbon in Portugal was destroyed by an earthquake, a tidal wave, and several fires. Can that possibly be a punishment from God? The study of evil moved away from theology, and distraught philosophers attributed evil to man. To reason.' He finished his drink. 'Whatever's in that house is evil in the premodern sense. A natural evil. Like an earthquake.'

'It killed the priest,' Emilia said.

'Interesting that you say that. You think it killed the priest?'

'It's not an earthquake,' she said. 'It's malicious. It toys with you.'

'If you think it's malicious,' Lucas said, 'why did it keep its word with Pauline?'

'Why would you lie to her about your parents?' Joaquin said. He gestured towards Michelle. 'So she'd feel sorry for you?' He crossed his legs, ice clinking like bells in his drink. 'If that were me, I wouldn't even say anything like that. I wouldn't want to attract bad fortune.'

Emilia scoffed. 'Is that how that works?'

Joaquin looked at Emilia. 'You're lucky to have the parents that you have and to have them both still alive.'

'I'd like it if it stayed that way,' Emilia said.

'Tell me you understand how lucky you are,' Joaquin said. 'If you had just let us get on with it and didn't interfere with Alma—'

'You think Pauline is having the time of her life, right?' Emilia said. 'You think you'd be able to sleep at night, if you did what she did?'

Lucas piped up, 'If it meant keeping my mother alive, why not?'

'You don't know that. You don't mean that.'

'Imagine a government official who takes money from the poorest families,' Lucas said. 'Lives a lavish lifestyle while everyone else starves. Lives rich, dies rich. He does his evil deeds, and yet he lives the good life, with absolutely no repercussions. You see it all the time. That's evil in the modern sense. So yes, I think Pauline is having a ball right now, Lia.'

'You keep saying you did it to help Alma,' Joaquin said, 'but where were you afterwards? You just discarded her.

You discarded all of us.' He shook his head. 'At least the priest had an excuse.'

'Don't you dare make me out to be the villain here,' Emilia said.

'Do you know how my father died?' Joaquin asked.

Emilia sighed deeply, exhausted, her legs shaking. 'You said it was an accident.'

Joaquin nodded. 'He hit his head on the kitchen sink as he fell. He was drunk, but that fall made him sober up really fast. He knew he was hurt. He knew it was a bad injury. He couldn't move his legs.' He gestured with his hand. 'Blood flowing in sheets down his face.'

'You don't have to talk about this,' Lucas mumbled.

'It was the middle of the night but the noise in the kitchen woke me up,' Joaquin continued, undeterred. 'I saw him fall. I saw his forehead split open. I stood by the sink while he lay on the floor, asking me for help. He was suddenly—' He paused at this point, remembering, watching the scene unfold in his mind's eye. '—he was suddenly the father I remembered when I was young, when my mother was still alive. Tender. Gentle. He kept saying, 'Son, please help me up.' He was afraid. There was so much blood. Then he started slurring his words. Do you know what I did?'

Lucas said again, louder this time, 'You don't have to talk about this.'

Emilia took a deep breath. In, out. 'What did you do, Joaquin?'

'Nothing,' he replied. 'That's what I did, Lia. I just stood there, watching him beg. For forty-seven minutes.' He knocked back his drink. 'I watched him die.' He turned to Lucas. 'Remember what Sophie said when she came to your house with Alma that night? Lia, I told you this. Do you remember?'

'I'm so sorry,' Emilia said.

'Sophie said my father will kill me, or I will kill him,' he said, 'One or the other, nothing else. Do you remember now?'

'I'm so sorry.' What else could she say? She remembered standing with Joaquin outside Lucas' house that warm evening, enveloped by the scent of sampaguita, the imagination of disaster.

Do you think you could ever kill someone?

No. And I don't think you can do something like that too.

Joaquin standing in the kitchen, watching the father he hated fade away. Watching himself fade away. How could that not break you?

She started to cry. 'I'm so, so, so sorry.'

Joaquin slapped an open palm on his thigh, the sound making her jump. 'Stop saying you're sorry!'

'Listen,' Lucas said, holding his hands up, his plea swallowed and spit out in a room that would not listen.

'If you really cared,' Joaquin told Emilia, 'you wouldn't have run away. You wouldn't have run away with Alma.'

Emilia turned to Sofia, but Sofia just looked back at her, cold and silent.

'Can you hear yourselves?' Emilia said. 'You talk about Alma like you cared about her, but you wanted to kill her. You wanted to kill her. You think you'd be able to live with yourselves if you went through with it?'

'She wanted to do it,' Joaquin said.

'You keep telling yourself that.'

That evening, on the day her father miraculously got better, Emilia waited for Joaquin outside the wet market. She sat on a wooden bench among passengers waiting for their boxed goods to be carted to the tricycles. The sky slowly turned the colour of honey. She remembered every detail of the last good day on earth, the wind blowing her hair into her eyes, the bench creaking with her every tiny move, the tricycles whizzing out of the passenger terminal. She watched the store owners fold their tables, roll down their steel shutters. When Joaquin emerged from the market's ever-darkening corridor, he looked surprised, then worried. He signalled to her with his head, *Over here.*

They stood by the Burger Machine where Emilia would buy her roast beef sandwich, her little treat after dealing with annoying customers and helping her parents at the store. How far away those days seemed now. The stall attendant was cleaning the grill, preparing to close, looking like he was already dead inside.

'What's wrong?' Joaquin's arms and hands smelled like mentholated soap, his temples like peppermint oil, the scent minty and sharp.

'Nothing's wrong,' she said. 'I don't know. My father's feeling better.'

'What?' He smiled. 'That's good. I mean, I don't even know what was happening in the first place. You won't tell me. Was it serious?'

'He was dying,' she said, distracted by the sound of metal scraping against metal, the Burger Machine attendant removing strips of meat from the grill. Joaquin touched her arm, pushed her away to a quieter corner.

'What did you say?'

'I spoke to it,' Emilia said. 'That thing. It would visit me looking like Miss Cardenas.'

Joaquin was silent.

'I bargained with it.'

'Bargained?' So *that* he found surprising.

'I wanted proof,' she said. 'Now my father is better.'

Joaquin was quiet again.

She said, 'It visited you, too, didn't it.'

'You bargained,' he said, looking pained. 'Why would you even speak to it?' He was staring off into the distance. She followed his gaze. There was a woman wearing a black dress squeezing into a tricycle with a large, black dog.

'I wanted to make sure,' she said.

'What are you saying now?' he said. 'You were screaming at us not to go there, to stay away from Sofia, you rushed to Lucas' to tell us not to listen to her, you fought with Lucas at every turn, and now—'

'I just want this to be over,' she found herself saying. The woman scratched the dog's head. Both the woman and the dog were staring at her. She felt goosebumps rise on her arms. 'We need to go to that house.'

They could have taken a tricycle, but Joaquin insisted that they walk. Emilia wondered if he was trying to bide his time, to give them both a chance to turn back, to not doom themselves. It took almost half an hour to get there. She only spoke once, just to ask, once again, 'What did Sofia say about Alma?' A question that had been gnawing at her. But Joaquin couldn't remember.

She was shocked to see Sofia, Alma, and Lucas already there, standing in the tall grass. Behind them, the decaying house loomed, door like a mouth waiting to swallow them whole.

'What did I tell you, Joaquin?' Sofia, sounding victorious, called out as they approached. 'I told you she'll come to you.'

'What?' Emilia came of her own volition but now she felt trapped, a black goat pulling at its leash.

'I was hoping Sophie was wrong,' Joaquin said.

Emilia walked up to Alma, who looked pale and in pain, her greasy hair tied in a ponytail. Emilia placed a hand on her back, felt her vibrating beneath her palm.

'I'm cold,' Alma said. 'I'm always cold now.' She touched her ponytail. 'And my hair keeps falling in clumps, so I—'

'It will be over soon,' Sofia said, grabbing Alma's wrist and walking with her up to the house.

Lucas had not said a word. Emilia walked between the two boys, like a prisoner between her guards. But she chose to be here. She chose to be here. Didn't she choose to be here?

'What's going to happen to Alma if we don't go through with this?' Emilia said, stopping this procession dead in its tracks.

'Lia,' Lucas said. Now he speaks? Alma glanced over her shoulder, but Sofia didn't even stop to look back, pushing onward through the grass, dragging Alma behind her.

'Why won't you tell us, Sophie?' Emilia said. But then they were through the door and inside the house, the revulsion like a gag pushing the words back down her throat. Across the entrance, right smack in the middle, the very first thing they saw as they walked through the doorway, was the mannequin sitting on a chair, dressed in white, covered from head to foot with a black veil. The way Pauline had left it.

It was just four walls and a roof, but didn't this feel like a buried altar, a dark church they weren't meant to see? It took all of her strength not to bolt and leave them all behind.

Lucas stared long and hard at the figure on the chair. 'Is that the mannequin from my father's office?' he asked Emilia.

Sofia sat on the floor with a piece of chalk, drawing the circle, the symbols. The wrongness of it. That was the point when they should have all run away, but they didn't.

Folie à plusieurs. The madness of many.

Alma touched her ears. 'The music stopped,' she said. She started to laugh. 'The music stopped, Lia.'

But no matter how willing they were, or how ready they felt, nothing could have prepared them for the sight of an inanimate object suddenly coming to life, that sharp intake of breath, the plastic mouth opening with a gasp, the rubber limbs twitching then settling.

Alma screamed through the whole ordeal. Emilia clapped her hands over her ears, shut her eyes tight. She could hear Joaquin and Lucas sobbing in the darkness.

Silence as the visitor settled in its vessel, the mannequin's head cocked as if it were waiting for something to happen. Waiting, waiting—

They had all fallen to their knees, facing this veiled altar.

How could any of them deny this now, now that they had seen it with their own two eyes?

'What happens now?' Alma squeaked.

Sofia turned and reached out an arm towards her. 'Come here.'

This was it, then, the answer to the question that had been eating Emilia inside out.

What did Sofia say about Alma?

Nothing, because Alma had no future.

'No,' Emilia said.

'We've talked about this,' Sofia said. 'It's all right, Lia.'

'She just needs a bit of my blood,' Alma said to her, a nurse placating a hysterical child. 'She just needs to cut across my palm. It would be over in a second.'

'Is that what you told her?' Emilia now on her feet, lifting Alma with her. Emilia could feel the sharp edges of Alma's shoulder bones beneath her shirt. She screamed at Sofia, 'Is that the lie you told her, so she'd come with you here?'

'I just want my family to be safe,' Alma said. 'Don't you want that? I just want this to be over.'

'Alma, she is going to kill you.'

Emilia watched several reactions flit across Alma's face: confusion, amusement, shock. Horror. 'What?' She turned to Sofia. 'What is she talking about?'

'Remember?' Emilia said, turning Alma's face so she would look at her instead. 'Remember what I said about Pauline and Miss Cardenas?'

Everyone else was now on their feet, closing in.

'Yes, but Sophie said—'

'She's a liar.'

'Sophie said it would be different this time.'

'We need to go,' Emilia said, but it was as if she were screaming in a storm, her voice lost in the din. 'Joaquin?' she called, grabbing their arms. Pleading. She felt as if she were in free-fall. 'Lucas?' She tugged at Alma's arm. 'We need to go. Please.'

'Sophie would never hurt any of us like that,' Alma said. 'Right?'

Emilia grabbed Alma by the hand and tried to bolt out of the house. Sofia screamed after them. Freedom was so near, they just needed to cross the threshold—

An impact that pushed the air out of her lungs. She fell to the floor and was flipped over to her back, Sofia grabbing her so violently by her shirt sleeve that it ripped in half. Pain exploding outward from the side of her face as Sofia slapped her.

'We don't have time for this,' Sofia said, pinning her down. 'I am trying to help you. Don't you understand?'

She could feel Sofia's heart beating through her chest like a trapped bird, could hear her breathing rapidly. She turned her head and saw Lucas and Joaquin in a corner of the room holding Alma's arms. She was crying, thrashing wildly between them. Lucas made a fist, threw his arm back—

Emilia felt the floor quiver as Lucas' fist made impact and Alma fell to the floor. She fell in front of the veiled form, which was still breathing, watching, waiting.

Sofia moved away from Emilia to see what was happening, and Emilia sat up, lifting her hands to cover her mouth. Alma's shoulders shook as she sobbed, face turned to the floor.

'Oh, God,' Joaquin said.

'I was,' Lucas sputtered. 'I didn't mean to—I was just trying to get her to stay still.' He moved towards Alma, reached out a hand—

'Don't you touch her,' Emilia said.

Lucas looked at her as though she had just stabbed him. 'I didn't mean to,' he said. 'Please. Lia. Joaquin.'

Joaquin was crying without a sound, the tears rolling down his cheeks. Emilia turned to him, gave him a look: *Do you see now?* But he looked resigned, the fight already leaving him.

Everything seems easy when you're talking hypothetically. But they had now all moved away from the realm of theory. One of them had hit their friend, and they were all still here, the world had not exploded, what could stop them now from moving forward, from doing more?

Emilia crawled to where Alma had fallen. Alma, suddenly mute and expressionless, lay on the floor on her back, eyes to the ceiling. The corner of her lip was cut open and bleeding.

Emilia could see blood vessels crawling across her right eye, turning her sclera red, the skin around it looking swollen and tender. 'Al?' she said. 'Are you okay?'

'My head hurts,' Alma said. She cried out when Emilia touched her temple.

Emilia could feel herself disintegrating, but she held on, she held on. 'I think she's badly hurt,' she said. 'We can take her to the hospital. We can still stop this, Lucas.'

Alma tilted her head, as though listening intently to someone.

'Lucas!' Emilia shouted, trying to get his attention. He knelt next to her, looking lost. 'Listen. I won't tell them you hit her.'

'I didn't mean to,' he said again.

'Lucas, you need to help me.'

'It's okay,' Alma said. 'I'm ready.'

'What?'

'It told me that it has to be me.'

'Hold her down,' Sofia said.

Emilia moved back in shock as they closed in: Joaquin on his knees with his hands on Alma's ankles, right above her shoes scuffed with grass and dirt. Lucas' shaking hand on her left wrist. Sofia kneeling by Alma's head with a knife, her head between her knees. One side of Alma's face already starting to darken as blood pooled beneath her skin.

Emilia stayed in a corner.

'Come here, Lia,' Sofia said.

Alma whimpered.

'Come here,' Sofia said again. 'Alma understands what we need to do.'

'It's okay,' Alma said, lifting her right hand from the floor, beckoning her. 'You need to be a part of this.'

After a moment, Emilia inched forward on the floor, hands on Alma's right arm, kneeling across from Lucas who could not look at her, all the while thinking: *How can this be happening? How can this be happening?*

Sofia had closed her eyes, holding the knife with both hands against her chest. Behind her, the mannequin beneath the veil breathed in, out. In, out. Emilia remembered the night she first saw Sofia with a knife like this. Alma, wide-eyed: *She's got a knife, a knife, a knife.* Sofia's father screaming, tangled up in bloody bedsheets on the bedroom floor.

'This is what you want?' Emilia whispered to Alma.

'Yes,' she whispered back.

'You're not thinking straight.'

'It's okay.'

'Al, they've already hurt you. You're going to die here.'

'Will you please just stop,' Joaquin said. 'Just stop.'

'Al,' Lucas said. 'Alma, I'm sorry.'

'Shut your mouth,' Joaquin said.

Emilia looked up at Joaquin in wonder.

A crack in the façade.

This wasn't set in stone. This could all still fall apart.

Lucas rocking on his knees: 'Just get on with it. Please.'

Alma crying: 'I'm ready. I'm ready.'

'Why did you agree to this?' Emilia said. 'Why does it have to be you?'

'It told me that it has to be me,' Alma said. 'There's no one else. We have no choice.'

There were tear stains on her face, but Alma was no longer crying. She had fallen silent. She looked like someone who had held on for as long as she could to the cliff face, and now she had allowed herself to fall.

Desperate, Emilia leaned down and whispered the first wild idea that came to mind: 'What if I can find someone else? A stranger? So you don't have to die?'

An intake of breath from the mannequin, hands raised beneath the black veil, a measured movement, like a door slowly opening.

The hope in Alma's eyes that only Emilia saw, that would haunt her for the rest of her days. But it was the only answer she needed.

'It's time,' Sofia said, opening her eyes. She raised the knife above her head, and with a roar Emilia surged forward, pushing Sofia down and punching her, the knife falling somewhere with a tinny clang, Joaquin and Lucas loosening their grip in their shock.

'Run!' Emilia shouted, putting her arms around Alma and pushing her up and out, her hand throbbing from the impact with Sofia's cheek, wind cooling the hot tears streaming down their faces as they ran through the grass, Sofia screaming in anguish behind them, 'No, no, what have you done—'

Alma looking back and stumbling, screaming in terror.

'What?' They could never stop. Emilia lifted her up and hurried her along, not daring to look back to see if Lucas and Joaquin had followed them. They needed to keep running, they needed to put as much distance between them and whatever it was in that house.

But Alma was saying something, holding her hands up to her eyes.

'Al, what did you say? What did you say?'

Alma screaming at the top of her lungs that she can't see, 'Lia, I can't see, I can't see. I can't see.'

A small crowd formed around them in the town square. Alma could not stop screaming. Emilia placed her hands on her face and whispered, 'Alma, stop. Stop. We've gotten away. You're safe now.'

Both of Alma's eyes were now bloodshot, unable to focus. A dark bruise blooming around her right eye. 'I can't see, Lia.'

Though it was full night, they were standing right beneath the neon sign of a pharmacy, the bright glow washing everything in blue and yellow light. 'Nothing at all? Not even a blurred shape?'

'There's nothing, it's just dark,' Alma said, shivering. 'I'm scared.'

Emilia remembered them as children in the school toolshed, seeing danger lurking in the shadows. How terrified Alma must have felt. She pulled her close, let her cry into her shoulder.

'Did something happen to your friend?' someone asked from the crowd. Another said, 'It looks like someone hit her in the face.'

An older woman touched Emilia's arm. 'Did someone hurt her, hija?'

Wasn't this where she began rewriting their history? 'I just found her walking around like this,' Emilia responded. 'She said she can't see.'

'But she wasn't blind before?'

'No. I think it just happened.'

Murmurs, shocked gasps from the crowd.

'I think we should take you to a doctor,' said the woman, directing them to a tricycle.

'Do you think a local hospital can handle her case?' a voice retorted. 'The girl can't see.'

'Can a punch make you blind?' someone wondered out loud.

What do you tell the parents of a girl who had suddenly become blind overnight? What explanation would suffice? Mr and Mrs Bartolome rushed to the hospital, demanding answers. Emilia stuck to her story: she found Alma walking around town, screaming that she could no longer see. She didn't know what happened, she couldn't explain it, I'm sorry, I don't know what else to say.

Mrs Bartolome took Emilia aside in the emergency room and asked her again where she found Alma.

'I told you, Tita, she was just walking—'

'Not on the ground?' Her voice shaking. 'Not—Did she have her clothes on? When you found her? You both have grass on your jeans.'

'I found her in a field. She was fully clothed, Tita. She was just disoriented.' She knew what Mrs Bartolome was asking. 'She wasn't hurt, not like that.'

'But she has a big bruise on her face,' she said. 'If you know who did this to her, you better tell me now.'

Lucas sitting on the edge of his bed, weighing his worth. *I never thought I was violent. I never thought I could hurt someone like that, but I did.*

The floor vibrating as Alma fell, and despite their tears and their horror, all they did was hold her down.

'I don't know, Tita,' she said. 'I'm telling you the truth.'

A day later, paramedics in the city were lifting Emilia's parents out from the wreckage of a bus crash.

Her father fell sick again after his one day of bliss, taking a turn for the worse. Her parents were on their way to a hospital recommended by her father's doctor. They took public transportation because they didn't own a car. In the end, her parents managed to arrive at the hospital they had meant to go to, their original destination—an insight that would make Emilia darkly laugh one moment and cry the next—but now as ICU patients.

'You could have told me,' Lucas said. 'I would have lent you my father's car. I could have even driven your parents.'

He and Joaquin would visit her in the hospital, bring her food and water, help her with lining up for paperwork, offer to stay overnight so she could sleep in her own bed. She never wanted to see them again, but she was too tired to refuse help. There was no one else. It was too overwhelming. She had read about ICU psychosis, in which ICU patients experienced disorientation, anxiety, extreme agitation. Saw or heard things that were not there. She was not the one hooked up to machines, but she could already feel her mind fraying, the beeps and blips invading her sleep, along with Miss Cardenas looking at her with disappointment. *Now what have you done, you silly goat?*

They were sitting in a waiting area outside the ICU. Joaquin had handed her a ham and cheese sandwich, but she couldn't eat. The despair in the air was so palpable it felt as if she was also ingesting other people's miseries by the mouthful.

'I didn't even know they were going to the city,' Emilia said. 'My mother panicked because my father got so much worse.'

'But you said it wasn't that serious, according to the doctor,' Lucas said.

'They said it was intestinal obstruction,' she said. 'A benign tumour. It caused him a lot of pain, but it could have been easily fixed with surgery.'

Her father got pinned badly in the crash, so the doctors had to amputate his legs. Wheelchair users the world over lived a full life, but after the accident, something more than his legs broke within her father. He couldn't get past the loss, couldn't feel whole. They shouldn't have rushed to the hospital in the city, he would think, every day. What was a bit of pain compared to a lifetime of dependence? Her mother would blame herself in the years that followed, and eventually, his father would blame her too. It was easy for him to trace causation. If they had not gone on that bus, they wouldn't be in an accident, his legs wouldn't be shredded by metal and asphalt, and he would still be able to walk. He would still have their house, their business, his old life that was not perfect but of which he was proud. It was all he could think about, even after they moved up north so they could be surrounded by family. Before Emilia refused all contact, she had screamed over the phone that she wished they would just separate instead of turning into miserable monsters together. But she knew he was dependent on her mother, knew her mother would never leave him.

At her lowest point, Emilia found herself telling her parents, 'Sometimes I wish you both just died.'

Some words you could never take back.

'So he wasn't dying after all?' Joaquin said.

My father is dying, isn't he? Emilia had played this scene over and over in her head. The thing wearing Miss Cardenas' face—did she say yes to this question? Did she say anything at all?

'Why would he be?' Lucas said. 'Wasn't he feeling much better the day before the accident? Good as new, Lia had said.'

Joaquin and Emilia shared a look. *You bargained.* There was pain on his face.

All that, only to be tricked.

'He was feeling much better before the accident,' Emilia said.

'Thank goodness you weren't on the bus with them,' Lucas said. He cleared his throat. 'Sophie and Al say hi, by the way.'

She could see that the madness had lifted, somewhat, but Lucas and Joaquin still talked about that night and what happened with Alma as if it were just a mundane errand that went awry.

'You're still talking to them?' Emilia said.

'Of course,' Joaquin said. 'Why wouldn't we be?'

'They're worried about you,' Lucas said.

'Are they?' Emilia said.

'Sophie wanted to visit and help out, but, you know, she's still taking care of her father.'

'And she's sick now too,' Joaquin added. 'She said everything she ate, she just threw right up.'

'Good,' Emilia said, making them turn away from her. 'I don't need her help.'

'Don't be like that,' Lucas said. 'She's still your friend.'

'Oh, okay,' Emilia said. 'Were you thinking that when you punched Alma so hard her eye turned red?'

She had raised her voice, making people in the waiting area turn their heads.

'Lia, please,' Joaquin said.

Lucas told her about his dream, a visitor wearing his dying mother's face. 'We could have left you out of it,' he said. 'But we wanted you to be safe too. And now—'

'And now what?' she said. 'Now look what happened to my parents.'

Lucas looked horrified. 'No, that's not what I—'

'Are you saying this is my fault?'

'Lia—'

Emilia swatted his hand away. 'Go to hell.'

And yet, in her darkest hours in the ICU, she would find herself thinking, *Did I cause this?*

She never confessed this to anyone, but one night, while sitting alone in the hospital cafeteria, wondering once again if her parents would recover or die in the night, she decided to dial Pauline's mobile number.

She wasn't even sure it was still an active number, but it began to ring, to her surprise.

'Hello?' The voice that answered was so cheerful. It sounded like a much younger version of Pauline, happy and open, with no worries in the world.

'Pauline?' she said, her chest aching.

The voice stayed silent. But whoever it was stayed on the line, and so did Emilia, trying hard to keep it together.

'I know what you did,' Emilia said.

Still nothing. Emilia thought she could hear a faint breeze through an open window, cars passing by, honks and beeps from a nearby street.

'I wasn't sure before,' Emilia continued, 'but now I know, because Sofia tried to do it too. To Alma.'

The person on the other line breathing in, breathing out. 'But I stopped it.'

No response.

'Tell me I did the right thing.'

Emilia felt as alone as she felt in that house, and in the ICU where her parents lay between living and dying. Rooms where no one could hear her.

When the voice on the other line continued to stay silent, Emilia said, 'You meant to kill me, didn't you? When you took me there? Would you have been able to do that? To hurt me and just walk away?'

'No,' the voice said, and Emilia stopped breathing. 'That's why I tried again, with someone else. You can just try again.'

Emilia suddenly didn't know what else to say.

'Do you know the worst thing anyone's ever said to me after my sister died?' the voice asked, and now Emilia was sure she was speaking to Pauline.

'What did they say?'

'"Do not conform to the pattern of this world",' Pauline replied. 'That's from Romans. I'm sure Catholic school boy Lucas could recite this by heart. "Do not conform to the pattern of this world, but be transformed by the renewing of your mind. Then you will be able to test and approve what God's will is—his good, pleasing, and perfect will."'

Tears were falling from Emilia's eyes. 'Pau.'

Pauline continued, '"Beloved, do not let this one thing escape your notice: With the Lord, a day is like a thousand years, and a thousand years are like a day. The Lord is not slow to fulfil His promise as some understand slowness."' She sighed deeply. 'That's the worst thing anyone's ever said to me. Is there a bigger plan here that I don't understand, that involves my sister having to die the way she did? Maybe. Who knows. But I don't want to fucking hear it.'

'Pauline, I miss you,' Emilia said.

No response.

'Why us?' Emilia said. 'Why did this happen to us?'

'You know the answer to that,' Pauline said. 'Why you? Why not you?'

A beep, and the call was over.

Emilia visited Alma in the hospital just once. She found it bewildering to watch her friend turn her head towards every little sound, her eyes bright but unfocused. Emilia closed her eyes as the nurses got her friend ready, imagining what it must be like for her. The soft purr of the bed as it was elevated, the clack of the side rails being lifted, Alma's warm fingers on her wrist. 'You're here.'

She opened her eyes. 'Hi, Al.'

'I heard about your parents,' Alma said, holding her hand. An intimate gesture, touch to stand in for her sight. What was her hand telling Alma now?

'We're cursed now, aren't we?' Alma said.

'You can't believe that,' Emilia said. 'You heard the doctor. There's nothing wrong with your eyes.'

'It doesn't matter what I believe,' Alma said. 'It's clearly happening.'

'It's just a story we told each other.'

She frowned. 'You saw what I saw.'

Emilia said nothing.

'You said,' Alma began, pulling at her hand, pulling her closer, pushing her to respond, 'you said we can find someone else. A stranger.'

'Yes,' Emilia said. Gently, gently, she pulled her hand back. Alma looked like someone lost at sea, turning her head this way, that way. 'It's okay, Al. I'm right here.'

'Will you do it?' Alma asked. 'Will you find someone else?'

What could she say to stop the look of panic invading Alma's eyes? 'Yes.'

But she never visited her again.

Emilia poured more whisky in her glass, gulped it down, the alcohol sliding like fire down her throat.

'You think you saved her, but you just prolonged her death,' Joaquin said. 'How is that a gift?'

'Don't you dare blame this on me.'

'Where were you when Sofia got sick?' he said. 'When Lucas' mother died? You even sent away your parents. We're the ones who had to live in the aftermath.'

'I told you not to go in that house,' she shouted. 'I begged you.'

'Then you came to me and begged that we go,' Joaquin said. He pointed at Michelle, sleeping sweetly, chest rising and falling in a steady rhythm. 'Why did you bring her here? Why did you show her the house?'

'I didn't.' She reached out to touch Michelle's arm, as though to protect her, shield her from the onslaught.

'Liar.'

'Oh, God. I didn't show her the house. We just got lost.' There was something wrong. The room was spinning.

'No, you didn't,' Joaquin said. 'You knew exactly where to turn.'

Emilia sat back down. She brushed against Michelle's limp arm. She could see Lucas sitting on the edge of his seat, hands loosely clasped. Waiting.

'There is so little now to be happy about,' Sofia said, speaking for the first time in a long time. 'But there are days when I hear a song I like, or I have a cup of good coffee, or I read a good book, and I forget, for a moment, everything that has happened. And I get so giddy, so unbelievably, incredibly happy. After all we have done, after everything we've allowed to happen, I'm still given these moments. It hardly seems fair, but I accept them, and I am grateful. I am so grateful. I want that for you too.'

'No,' Emilia said, fighting hard to keep her eyes open. 'There's something wrong. It's—'

Michelle's glass on the floor next to Lucas's feet.

Emilia thought back to their meal, Joaquin emerging with a pill box, the tiny plastic window marked *Saturday*, Sofia's multicoloured pills.

They had put something in their drink.

'It's time,' Lucas said, and stood up.

'Alma kept saying you will find someone else.'

When Emilia came to in the darkness next to Michelle, the sound of rain surrounding her, she thought she was still sitting on the sofa. She couldn't move her hands or feet, and realized with confusion that they were bound with packaging tape. What was happening? She turned her head and saw a slash of tape over Michelle's mouth. Michelle was still sleeping, leaning against Lucas.

They were not on the sofa. They were in the backseat of Michelle's car, Michelle sitting between her and Lucas, with Joaquin behind the wheel and Sofia on the passenger seat.

Lucas looked at Emilia with what seemed to be pity. *This stupid rain and this stupid car,* she had said, and Lucas was about to tell her: *About the car—*

Joaquin calling her father's friend, the mechanic.

Was there even really a mechanic?

She began to cry. They didn't put tape over her mouth. First, a betrayal that cut her, and suddenly this faith that, after everything, she would still be on their side, that she would not scream to hurt them.

'I knew you'd come back,' Sofia said. 'The boys didn't think you would, but I did.'

They parked on the side of the road. Her friends were even wearing raincoats. Did they start planning this the moment they saw her and Michelle arrive at the wake? Lucas got out of the car, his shoes squelching in wet grass, and came over to Emilia's side. He opened the door and crouched down to cut the tape binding her.

She should kick him. She should be fighting. But she felt weak all over, already defeated.

Sofia walked across the field, followed by Joaquin carrying Michelle in his arms, as if she were an animal about to be slaughtered. Which she was, wasn't she? She remembered Pauline's screaming goat, digging its heels, pulling at its leash.

Lucas held Emilia up, practically dragging her, at the tail end of this strange procession. The cold rain came as a shock.

'Please,' she said. How many years had she been saying this? 'Please don't do this.'

They entered the house again for the first time in twelve years. Everything covered in dust and thick cobwebs, even the veiled form sitting on its chair. Emilia gagged from the smell of rot.

Sofia's hand came away black when she tried to wipe dust off the floor. She drew the circle, the symbols, white chalk cutting through the black dust. Joaquin and Lucas lay Michelle on the floor, limbs still bound with tape.

They waited for whatever it was to walk through the doorway, for the vessel to come to life.

Rain lashed against the house and through the gaps in the walls.

Nothing was happening.

'I don't believe this,' Joaquin muttered. 'There must be something wrong with the symbols. Look again.'

Emilia felt hope blossom within her. 'What you offered wasn't enough to make it come to you, Sophie.'

'I've cut myself up to look like you,' Sofia said, addressing the veiled form. 'For years. For years and years. It should be enough.'

'Sophie,' Lucas said. 'You need to do something. She's starting to wake up.'

On the floor, Michelle's eyes moved rapidly beneath her eyelids, like a person dreaming.

'Just let us go,' Emilia said.

Sofia glanced at Michelle, at the tape over her hands and legs. 'We wanted to avoid the same mistakes, Lia,' she said. 'We didn't want anyone changing their minds, or running away, or crying in fear while waiting for the knife to fall. She'll fall asleep and never wake up in pain. A little mercy.'

Sofia took out her knife and cut the tape from Michelle's wrists and legs, and ripped it off her mouth.

She turned to the veiled form. 'But the suffering is the point, isn't it?' she whispered.

Michelle, groggy but awake now, muttered something unintelligible. Then: 'Em? What's going on? Where—'

Before Emilia could move or say anything, Sofia yanked Michelle up to a sitting position and turned her around to face the form on the chair. 'Watch.'

Emilia covered her ears and closed her eyes.

Michelle screamed as the mannequin became animate and the smell of rot and piss and bile intensified, as though its heart and lungs and liver and intestines, made from polymer and plastic, visible through decade-old chiffon and lace, suddenly became living flesh.

It wasn't like this before. Emilia found it hard to breathe.

Was there now an actual decaying body beneath that veil?

Sofia shouted orders. Joaquin and Lucas tried to hold Michelle down, but she was not Alma. Michelle was fighting hard, arching her back to pull away from their grip, to rip their arms off her body. Kicking her legs, shoes thumping on the floor. If Sofia tried to move the knife now, she would most likely stab Lucas or Joaquin. Emilia stayed in one corner, her body feeling heavy.

'Just hit her, Lucas,' Joaquin shouted.

Emilia watched them realize, as though for the first time, that they were about to take a life. The enormity of it.

'What?' Lucas said.

'Hit her so she'd stop moving,' Joaquin said, glaring at him. 'Just do it.'

'Hit her the way you hit Alma,' Emilia said. 'Do you remember that, Lucas? You hit her so hard her right eye turned red. Is that who you are?'

Joaquin glanced over his shoulder to glare at her. *How dare you?*

Lucas was the first to loosen his grip. 'This is—' He couldn't even finish his sentence. He looked shell-shocked. Michelle's arm whacked against his chest, and he lifted his arms to block the blows.

'No,' Sofia shouted. 'Just hold on, just hold on.'

Joaquin held Michelle down as she bucked beneath him, tears pouring down his face. 'Please, just stop moving,' he said.

Michelle screamed. The wind whistled across the field while the mannequin watched from its seat and took a steady breath. In, out. In, out.

Waiting.

Emilia thought of Michelle peering over her cubicle: *You're not eating lunch at your desk.* Was that only a day ago? Kindness that devolved into this horror.

'Just take me,' Emilia said.

Everyone stopped moving. Michelle took advantage of the distraction and squirmed away from under Joaquin and Sofia, crawling to the doorway, but Joaquin shook himself awake and caught up with her, grabbing her from behind.

Michelle couldn't fight any more. She whimpered and cradled her arms covered in scratches and bruises as Joaquin held her in place.

'We all want this to be over,' Emilia said. The floor creaked as she walked and knelt in front of Sofia. She grabbed Sofia's hand and guided her knife to her throat. 'Come on then.'

Lucas broke the small silence that followed. 'No,' he said. 'You can't do this. Sophie, this was not how this was supposed to go.'

'Lia,' Joaquin said. He couldn't say anything more.

'I wanted to save you,' Sofia said.

'I know,' Emilia said. The blade was so close it had started to nick her. She felt the sting, the tiny rivulet of blood dripping down her neck. Sofia's eyes were big and shiny with tears. 'Now I can save you.'

Sofia held the knife still.

'Can you tell my parents,' Emilia began. But there was so much to tell, and not enough words to tell it.

'Moral luck,' Sofia said, and laughed. 'If only we were somewhere else, sometime else. My biggest problem would have been how to get into a good college.'

Emilia laughed with her until the laughter turned into hiccupping sobs.

'If we weren't tested like this, we would have been so happy,' Sofia said.

But who was to be blamed? Sofia? Pauline? The truncheon that killed Mia? The hate that moved the truncheon? The cancer, the illness, the unforeseen? The unseen disturbed from slumber?

'I knew you'd come back. I always knew.' Sofia turned the knife around. Emilia touched the handle out of reflex and surprise. Sofia wrapped a hand around Emilia's wrist and guided her to plunge the knife into her own chest.

The surprised screams that followed drowned Emilia's thoughts. Sofia pulled the knife out, and the blood that gushed out of her felt warm—a sudden, suffocating river that drowned Emilia. She felt ice form in her throat as the cloying smell of perfume filled the room, as she watched the veiled form stand from the chair and levitate from the floor. Emilia lifted her head, watching its ascension, her swallowed scream an obstruction in her throat. The mannequin raised its hands, palms outward, as though giving them all a blessing.

Then slowly, slowly, its hands grabbed the black veil, lifting its covering up, up, up—its impossible mouth now visible, jaws moving as it attempted to speak.

Michelle screamed and broke away from Joaquin's grip, rushing out the door. Emilia felt someone grab her, and suddenly she was running headlong into the pouring rain between Joaquin and Lucas, the water drumming on her head and sluicing off her skin, washing away Sofia's blood.

Michelle was now running ahead of them all, towards her car.

Lucas looked back at the house over his shoulder and screamed, falling to his knees. They helped him up and kept running. They had to keep running. No one wanted to hear the veiled form speak. No one wanted to see the face it now wore.

Emilia wanted to look back, to see if whatever it was that dwelled in that house had followed them, but she dared not look back.

Michelle passed out before she could get to her car. Joaquin and Emilia lifted her off the wet grass and into the back seat. The rest of them climbed in as lightning streaked the sky, Lucas screaming with his hands over his eyes. Joaquin pushed him into the passenger seat and buckled him in.

Joaquin peeled out of the field and landed the car on the road with a loud thud.

Lucas was saying something they couldn't understand. 'What is it?' Joaquin said, glancing from the road to peer at his face, hand on his nape. 'Are you hurt?'

Lucas' eyes were bloodshot when he lowered his hands.

'I can't see,' he said. 'I can't see.'

The Emergency Room was filled to the rafters with patients with broken bones, lacerations. Emilia watched a family of five surround a gurney, a body covered with a white sheet, the top of the sheet covered in bright-red blood. A silence, then the eruption of tears. 'He was just crossing the street,' the mother bawled. A doctor telling the father that his other son was still alive, but they had to do the surgery now, he had to make some calls now, round up some blood donors. Now now now. The father, looking like a man at the foot of a landslide, not running, already accepting what was to come.

The doctor who approached Emilia looked confused. 'Where did your friend get this injury?' The diagnosis was corneal flash burn, a painful inflammation of the cornea. 'It's the kind of injury you get when the eyes get exposed to intense, bright light.'

Emilia pulled him to a corner, away from Lucas' earshot. 'Is this permanent?' she asked. 'Will he be able to see?'

'The injury is quite extensive, but the cornea can repair itself,' the doctor replied. He glanced at Lucas' chart. 'We're keeping him under observation for forty-eight hours.'

Not a yes, but not a no either. 'Okay.'

The doctor asked again, 'How did he get this injury, Miss?'

She didn't know what Lucas saw in the house when he looked back. What it was that was revealed to him. She and

Joaquin had asked in the car, but he refused to tell them, only responding with incoherent screams.

'I don't know,' she answered truthfully. 'How about my other friend, the woman who came in with us?'

Michelle was sitting on a cot in the emergency room, squinting at the tiny TV mounted on the wall in a corner. Face shiny and scrubbed clean. Eating instant noodles without a care in the world.

'One of the nurses got me this,' she said, holding up her ramen cup.

They had her change into a hospital gown, Michelle explained, tied her hair in a neat ponytail. Her wet ball of clothes streaked with mud and grass were in a plastic bag underneath the cot.

Emilia approached slowly, as if cornering a wild animal, but Michelle just smiled at her, looking peaceful. 'I'm okay. I just had a CT scan done.'

Emilia sat down on a plastic chair next to the cot. 'Why did they ask for a CT scan?'

Michelle slurped up some noodles. 'They want to check if I have a concussion,' she replied as she chewed. 'I know Joaquin told them I fell. But I don't remember anything at all.'

'You don't remember anything?'

She nodded. 'Hence the CT scan.' She ate some more, wiped her mouth with the back of her hand.

'What's the last thing you remember?' Emilia asked.

'We were drinking. In Sophie's house. I didn't even drink that much. I can usually handle my liquor, you know? I don't know what happened after.'

'You did fall,' Emilia said, slowly, as if she were knitting the words together. 'You ran outside.'

'My God.' Michelle looked mortified. 'How embarrassing. And during your friend's wake too. I'm so sorry.' She frowned. 'I really don't think I drank that much. I've never had an episode like this. I usually just get talkative.'

'But you're okay? Right? You're okay?'

Michelle shrugged. 'I don't know. I feel all right.' She was about to reach down to put her empty noodle cup on the floor when Emilia intercepted to help. 'Oh. Thanks. I'm just hungry, and a bit woozy. But the good news is, the traffic on NLEX is moving again and my family's coming over to pick me up.'

'You're okay,' Emilia said again. But was she really? Was the memory erased or would it return, years later, the smell of rot covered by the smell of perfume, three strangers holding her down, a veiled form stalking her in her nightmares?

'Do you want to come with us?' Michelle was saying. 'I'm dying for some danggit. I'm waiting for the doctor to return with the results but I'm pretty sure I don't have a concussion, just the hangover of the century. They'll let me leave soon. Do you know how Joaquin managed to fix my car, by the way? Wait. What's wrong?'

'I didn't mean you any harm,' Emilia said.

'I know that, silly.'

'I never wanted to hurt you.'

A confused smile from Michelle. 'What are you even talking about?'

Emilia lifted her hands to her face and cried. Shoulders shaking, hot tears flowing down her face and dripping from her cheeks.

'Whoa,' she heard Michelle say. 'What's going on?' She felt Michelle's hand on her head, her fingers running through her hair. 'It's okay, Em,' she murmured. 'I just got drunk. It's not a big deal, really.'

Joaquin filled out all of the paperwork, and he and Emilia paid the deposit so Lucas could be given a private room.

After the nurses and the doctors and the credit officers left, Lucas spoke for the first time since they got to the hospital. His voice sounded hoarse.

'Are you both here?' Lucas said. The doctor had put dilating drops in his red-rimmed eyes, and his pupils looked bigger than normal, even in the dark room.

'We're here,' Joaquin said, throwing a towel over the lamp before turning it on. 'Does the light hurt?'

'No.'

'Can you see anything at all?'

'Some.'

Emilia smiled. 'Really? That's good. How many fingers am I holding up?'

'Two,' Lucas said.

Emilia, who wasn't holding up her hand, said, 'That's right.'

They turned away from each other, allowing the untruth to settle between them.

'Where's Michelle?'

'She's okay,' Emilia replied. 'Her family's on their way.' She glanced at Joaquin. 'She doesn't remember what happened.'

'At all?' Lucas said.

'No.'

'And—' He let out a choked sob, 'And Sophie?'

'Don't cry,' Joaquin said, even as he and Emilia started to whimper. 'You need to rest your eyes.' He paused before continuing, 'They'll probably find her tomorrow. After the rain.'

'They'll say horrible things about her,' Lucas said. 'They'll say her father got mutilated years ago and now she finally went insane and stabbed herself.'

'Stop,' Joaquin said, patting his knee. 'Stop.'

'They're just keeping you here for observation.' Emilia reached over to dry Lucas' eyes. 'One day, your sight will return. Okay? It did for Alma.'

Lucas cried harder. 'I don't want to end up like Alma.'

They fell silent and watched on, helpless, as Lucas wept.

'You won't,' Emilia said. She met Joaquin's weary eyes. 'We won't let that happen again.'

'What happens now?' Lucas asked. 'What do we do now?'

Joaquin sighed. 'Now,' he said, 'now, we enjoy our good fortune.'

Emilia reached out to take her friends' hands and held on to them like someone scrambling up the cliff face to safety.

Exhausted and soul-sick, Emilia closed her eyes and rested her head on the edge of Lucas' hospital bed.

A quick jolt, and suddenly she was on her feet, following a woman down a busy sidewalk. Emilia looked around her, at the tall buildings, the business suits, the designer bags carried by women now wearing flats, their stilettos stuffed in a canvas tote bag at the end of the workday. A city that was expensive but safe, expensive therefore safe, expensively safe.

Everything felt simultaneously strange and familiar, as things often do in dreams.

The woman looked back over a shoulder and smiled.
'Hurry up, Lia.'

It was Sofia.

In the room where Emilia lay sleeping, she knew Sofia
was dead, the rain washing away the carnage of her sacrifice.

But Emilia allowed herself to sink further into the
dream, to not question anything. 'Will you slow down?' she
told her friend.

Sofia walked fast, faster than her, and Emilia nearly lost her
breath trying to catch up. They crossed under an expressway
and emerged from its shadow onto the brightness of a wharf.
The water looked black, caged in by the corporate buildings,
the busy harbour, a sparkling bridge. There were no stars.

Emilia felt charmed by this, the black water, the bright lights
of wherever this was, but the charm came with a heaviness.

Was it possible to be both comforted and lonely at the
same time?

Sofia took her to a table outside a restaurant situated near
the water. There were birds circling above them, so high up
they were only white outlines against the sky. Sofia pointed
them out to her, amused.

This was the Sofia who got out, the Sofia who escaped
the narrative.

'How are things?' Sofia asked. 'How's Alma? How are
Lucas and Joaquin?'

Can't the dead be merciful and just tell Emilia their fates?

'They're okay,' Emilia said. 'They're all doing okay.'

Sofia seemed delighted. 'And you. You look well.'

Emilia ran her palms over the menu on the table, her
fingers tracing the gilded letters.

She wanted to say: I'm sure my being alive is a grave injustice.

She wanted to say: Please give me a house in the middle of nowhere, on a patch of land outside of time, where no one will hurt me, where I will hurt no one.

But instead, she said, 'I'll miss you so much, Sophie.'

Sofia, who had been staring at the birds, looked at her and frowned. 'What do you mean?' She laughed. 'I'm right here, stupid.'

Emilia swallowed a sob, willed the tears away. 'Of course,' she said. 'You're right. You are right here.'

She tried her hardest to stay in the twilight space between sleeping and waking, sitting by this nameless ocean, this table surrounded by the idle, mindless chatter of strangers, in front of her friend who was alive, who was living.

But morning was coming. She must allow it.

Author's Note & Acknowledgements

This novel is the result of many ideas I have been obsessed with for many years, some twisted to my own ends for storytelling purposes, but I would like to point to three concepts and some sources if readers would like to know more:

- The concepts of 'profane time' and 'sacred time' mentioned here are based on and inspired by Mircea Eliade's *The Sacred and the Profane: The Nature of Religion* (1st American ed., Harcourt, Brace, 1959).
- 'Moral luck' is a term introduced by Bernard Williams but some of the ideas presented here and discussed by the character Sofia are inspired by Thomas Nagel's essay on the topic published in 1979.
- The shuttlebox experiment mentioned here is based on the 1967 experiment that was part of psychologist Martin Seligman's research on 'learned helplessness'.

If it appears that I have misunderstood or misrepresented these concepts, the fault is all mine and not of the above experts.

This story has gone through many, many, *many* (so many) major and minor revisions. Early versions of some sections were read and discussed in creative writing workshops by members of my cohort at the University of Sydney. Those sections would be unrecognizable to them now in this final form, but I would like to thank them for their time and their thoughtful notes.

Thank you to Johanna, fellow Scorpio, occasional Newtown companion, and creative writing sounding board. (Writing is so hard! Why do we even do this?)

Thank you to Nora Nazerene Abu Bakar and the team at Penguin Random House Southeast Asia for believing in this novel.

Thank you, readers, old and new.

Thank you to my family, immediate and extended, for their love and support.

I would like to thank my circle of friends from high school who, miraculously, I'm still in touch with after all these years, scattered as we are across the globe, and who, thankfully, are doing much, *much* better than the characters in this novel: June, Ghia, Maricon, Richard, Sasa, and Grace.

This book is for Jaykie Lazarte, who knows I'm usually nicer than the characters I create.

Eliza Victoria